Trouble in Texas
A Summer Adventure

Mary Nolan Brown

PROMINENT
BOOKS
EDGE

Acknowledgments

No one creates without the help of others.

My Thanks to:

John Light Jr., Youth Services supervisor, Live Oak Public Libraries, Savannah, Georgia, for his insight and advice.

Ed Eckstrand for his creative and technical support.

Cecilia Morette for her help and encouragement.

Nancy Raines Day for her editing.

Members of Coastal Kids Writers and Illustrators and Senior Citizens Writers Circle critique groups for their support.

The late Morris Craig, publisher, The Monitor, Naples, Texas, for his interest and sharing copies of the newspaper.

Chapter 1

OMAHA, TEXAS
June 1944

Through the train window, Matt read the faded sign on the end of the building—"Omaha, Texas, Population 920." Across the street that ran beside the railroad track were a grocery store, a drugstore, a hardware store, and a bank. Beyond the bank was a vacant lot.

This was the summer Matt had hoped his mother would let him go to Comiskey Park to see the Chicago White Sox play. Instead, he was about as far from Comiskey Park as he could imagine.

He spied his grandparents, Grandpa in overalls and a wide-brimmed straw hat and Grandma in a flowered cotton housedress, waiting on the platform. They looked like Ma and Pa Kettle in the Saturday afternoon comedies at the movie theater. He was glad his friends back in Chicago couldn't see them.

"Boy, get a move on. They need to get this train on down the track," Grandpa said when Matt hung back as the conductor helped his mother off the train. "The Cotton Belt's got a schedule to keep."

Matt hesitated, breathed a sigh of resignation, and jumped from the bottom step to the gravel roadbed.

"We're so glad you can spend the summer with us, Matthew," Grandma said when he reached the platform, giving him a hug. He gave her a hug in return and mumbled something about being glad to be there. No fourteen-year-old boy really wants to be hugged—but they make allowances for grandmas.

He was glad Grandpa didn't try to hug him.

"The car's 'cross the street," Grandpa said, handing Matt one of the suitcases while he picked up the rest.

Matt looked to where a 1939 Chevrolet sedan was parked in front of the drugstore. Horses were tied to the rail next to the car. Two boys with ice cream cones came out of the drugstore, mounted the horses, and rode slowly down the street. Matt was disappointed. Whoever heard of cowboys eating ice cream cones?

Grandma joined Matt's mother in the back seat of the car. They began discussing the trip while Matt and Grandpa put the luggage in the trunk.

"How was school this year, Matthew?" Grandma asked when Matt was settled in the front seat beside Grandpa.

"Fine," he replied.

He couldn't think of anything else to say. He hadn't seen his grandparents since they had visited before his father was shipped overseas with his army unit. That was four years ago. He wondered if he'd feel this way when his father came home from the war.

Grandma seemed to understand and turned to Matt's mother. "How long can you stay?" she asked.

"I'll have to go back day after tomorrow," Mom replied. "I was able to take a few days off to bring Matt, but I have to be back at the hospital Friday. We're trying to get the wards ready in case there's an outbreak of polio again this summer."

"My friend Bob caught polio last summer, and he's still in the hospital in an iron lung," Matt said. "I've seen people in iron lungs in the news reel at the movies. It looks like they're in big tin cans with their heads sticking out one end."

"Well, I'm glad you can stay with us for the summer. It's healthier here," Grandma said. "I hear all the big city theaters and swimming pools are being closed for the summer because the health department doesn't want people crowding together and passing germs around. Makes me glad we don't have a movie theater and do have lots of open space and fresh air."

Matt counted the barbed-wire-strung fence posts along the side of the road as they passed. Across the fields, he could see trees growing on the banks of a creek. There was not a person in sight. He was going to spend the summer in a town with no movie theater and no baseball.

As they started around a curve in the road, two riders on horseback came galloping down the middle of the road straight at them. Grandpa put on the brakes, sending everyone sliding in their seats. Matt would have hit the windshield if Grandpa hadn't thrown his arm across Matt's chest.

The riders raced by—one on either side of the car—laughing and waving their hats in the air.

"Those dadburn Wilson boys are going to kill themselves or somebody else one of these days if they aren't careful," Grandpa exclaimed.

"They've pretty much run wild since their daddy's been gone," Grandma said. "Jean makes excuses for them every time they get in trouble. She says her boys aren't bad, they're just high-spirited."

"They've been lucky so far," Grandpa said. "I heard they were the ringleaders of the bunch that put Coach's Austin Healy on his front porch last Halloween. Coach had to take down the railing before he could get that car off the porch."

"And that wasn't all, those boys roped the tongue of the highway tar wagon and used their horses to pull the wagon up to the second floor of the school—put Tom Wright's heifer up there too. What a mess! It took most of a day to get that cow to walk down two flights of stairs. The boys thought it was a big joke. They're going to go too far one of these days."

Matt craned his neck for a better look at the riders, but all he could see was the cloud of dust their horses had left behind. Maybe the summer wasn't going to be so dull after all.

Chapter 2

A small black-and-white dog came from under the front porch when they pulled into the drive beside a one-story white house set back under tall oak trees. The dog shook itself from head to toe and began barking and jumping up and down.

"Would you just listen to Lady?" Grandma said. "She likes to greet everybody who comes on the place."

Matt didn't think that sounded like a greeting. It sounded downright unfriendly to him. Last summer, a neighbor's dog had gotten out of their fenced yard and chased him home. Matt didn't trust dogs after that.

Lady came running up to Matt as he got out of the car.

"Get away!" he yelled and backed away.

"Hey, now, Matthew, what's this all about?" Grandpa asked.

"I don't like dogs," Matt said.

To make matters worse, another dog came from the back of the house. It was bigger than Lady. It didn't bark at him; it just raised its head, looked around, sniffed the air, walked up on the front porch, and sprawled out in the shade.

"That's Duke," Grandpa said. "He's the boss. You'd better make friends with him."

Grandpa picked up the two suitcases and walked to the front door, leaving Matt to carry the other suitcase. Matt looked at the front door. To get there, he would have to walk between the dogs. Lady was standing by the door, watching him. Duke seemed to have gone to sleep, but Matt couldn't be sure.

Edging away from the car, Matt started toward the back of the house and the back door. Lady followed. On the back porch, he reached to open the screened door—it was latched.

"Somebody, let me in!" he yelled.

Matt glanced over his shoulder as Grandma opened the door. Lady was sitting with her head cocked to one side, and Duke was sitting beside her watching Matt.

"They were going to bite me!"

"No, they weren't," Grandma said. "They're just curious."

Grandpa, standing in the doorway to the kitchen, shook his head, turned, and walked toward the front of the house.

"This was your daddy's room," Granda said as she led Matt to a bedroom just off the kitchen. His suitcases were on the floor beside the chest of drawers. "Do you want me to help you unpack?"

"No'um," he answered, hesitating at the door.

"Well then, I'll finish getting supper on the table," she said.

Matt pulled out the top drawer of the chest of drawers to put his clothes away. There were things in the drawer—a bag of marbles, a pocketknife, some neatly folded red and blue bandanas, and a 4-H brochure. He looked at them for a minute before closing the drawer.

Try as he might, he couldn't imagine his father in this room. His mother shared the V-mail that came from his father. There were holes cut in the thin paper where the censors had clipped away anything they thought shouldn't be shared. After all, "Loose Lips Sink Ships," the posters on the post office wall, declared. But none of this made his father real to him.

Matt opened another drawer and began to put his clothes away. From the kitchen, he could hear the sounds of his grandmother preparing supper.

"Mom, what may I do to help?" he heard his mother ask.

"Everything is done, but you can set the table, Ann," Grandma replied.

"Dad didn't seem to be pleased to see us this afternoon. Is everything all right?" Mom asked.

"You know how hard it's been for everybody since the depression began. So many businesses closed, banks failed, and people lost their life savings. People panicked. Some banks closed when people started withdrawing their money. Our friend Henry Smith withdrew his life savings from the bank, put it in a box, and hid it under his bed. How safe do you think it was there? If many people had done that, our bank would have failed too."

"What happened?" Mom asked.

"Mr. Paulson, a rancher north of town, asked the bank president Mr. Randall to call a meeting of the people who had money in the bank. Everybody came."

"I imagine they were curious," Mom said.

"Oh, yes, they were. Mr. Paulson told the crowd he had faith in Mr. Randall and the bank. And to prove it, he gave ten thousand dollars in cash of his own money for Mr. Randall to deposit in the bank. He had two of his ranch hands with guns standing guard at the door. The guards and all the people at the meeting escorted Mr. Randall to the bank to put the money in the safe. After that, not a soul withdrew their accounts. Mr. Paulson saved the bank."

"What a relief that must have been," Mom said.

"It was, but it didn't solve all the problems," Grandma said. "We had to sell the cattle. Couldn't afford the extra feed or a hand to help with the chores. Oscar still believes everything would have been fine if Sam had stayed and worked the farm. Instead, he joined the army."

"Of course, I know his staying would have made it even harder. What with the depression and the freeze killing the peach orchard, having another family to support would have made it even harder. Times like this, there are no easy answers."

After supper, Matt went out on the front porch to be by himself. When his mother joined him, he didn't mention overhearing her conversation with Grandma.

"Mom, I don't want to stay here. Grandpa doesn't like me. Can't I go back with you?"

"Matt, I told you, Mrs. Johnson isn't well, and you can't stay with her during the day while I'm at work. I tried to find someone else but couldn't. Grandpa may be grumpy at times, but it looks like he and Grandma could use some help. And besides, I feel better with you being here for the summer. There may be another polio outbreak."

Matt sat on the porch steps until after dark. He didn't even go in when Grandma came to the door and asked if he'd like some dessert. His summer was ruined, and dessert wasn't going to make it any better.

*　　*　　*

He had trouble falling asleep that night. Strange sounds were coming in through the open window. Just as he was drifting off to sleep, he heard the distant whistle of a train. He wished he was on that train going home.

Matt wasn't quite sure where he was when he first awoke the next morning. It was still dark outside, but light shown under the bedroom door. Try as he might, he couldn't go back to sleep. The murmur of voices from the kitchen and the smell of bacon cooking were too much to endure. He struggled out of bed and into his clothes.

Grandpa was sitting at the table, drinking coffee when Matt walked into the kitchen. Grandma, with a big white apron tied over her bathrobe, was at the stove.

"Mornin', Matthew," Grandma said. "I hope we didn't wake you. Your mother's still asleep. I imagine she could use some extra rest after the long hours she keeps at the hospital. Your grandpa's already been out and milked Bonnie. You can help me gather the eggs later."

"Yes'um," said a sleepy-eyed Matt as he sat down at the table.

"Grandpa's already asked the blessin'," Grandma said as she set a plate of bacon and eggs in front of him.

Matt lifted the cloth on a basket of fresh, hot biscuits and helped himself to the large one. When he had finished eating, he leaned back in the chair and closed his eyes.

E-E-E-E-E-E-E hu-hu-hu-hu.

A horrible scream followed by deep groans rent the air. It was like nothing Matt had ever heard. He clutched the edge of the table and looked from his grandfather to his grandmother.

Didn't they hear it? He knew older folks didn't hear too well, but he was sure even a deaf person could hear that.

E-E-E-E-E-E hu-hu-hu-hu-hu.

There it was again! It seemed louder and closer than before. Matt didn't know whether to hide under the table or make a run for the bedroom.

Chapter 3

"Guess it's 'bout time to take care of Millie and Jack," Grandpa said, not even looking up from his plate. "They seem to think they're in charge 'round here."

He finished his breakfast, took a last drink of coffee, and stood up.

"Good breakfast, as usual," he said to Grandma. "Come on, Matthew, I'll introduce you to Millie and her crew."

Matt didn't move. He didn't want to meet anyone if it meant going outside where that horrible noise came from—a noise that only he seemed to hear. Just then he heard it again!

"Matt, don't just sit there!" Grandpa exclaimed. "Those mules are gettin' mighty impatient to be let out."

"Mules? Is that what's making all that noise?"

"Sure is," said Grandpa. "They let me know if they think I'm a little late letting them out in the mornin'."

Matt hesitated and then followed his grandfather out the back door. The sun was still below the horizon, but there was enough light for Matt to see the barn and a shed. A corral was attached to the barn. Matt stopped in his tracks. Silhouetted against the dawn were six of the largest animals he had ever seen. Their heads, with ears pointing forward toward Grandpa, were well above the top rail of the corral.

"This here's Millie, Jack, Dusty, John Henry, Jenny, and Joe. Millie's the boss, but Jack thinks he is. She reminds him every once in a while with a nip on his rump," Grandpa said. As he talked, he went to each mule in turn and stroked its nose and gave it a carrot from his pocket.

"They're smart and hard workers. People who use tractors are having a hard time gettin' gasoline, even with special ration stamps for farmers. But if you have a mule, you don't have to worry about gasoline."

As Grandpa moved toward the barn, Matt stood and looked at the mules. They seemed to be watching him. Their ears wiggled as if they were sending signals to each other. He jumped back when one of the mules extended its head over the rail and reached toward him.

"Joe's got a real sweet tooth. He was hoping you'd give him a lump of sugar. I give them carrots now that sugar's rationed," Grandpa said as he came out of the barn and opened the corral gate that led into the pasture. The mules turned away from Matt and broke for freedom.

"Where're they going?" asked Matt.

"They'll spend most of the day under the trees out of the heat. We've about five acres fenced. It goes down to the tree line over yonder by the creek. We used to run a few head of cattle, but now we keep only one milk cow."

Grandpa looked at Matt. "I don't suppose you've milked a cow."

"No, sir," Matt said. Not only had he not milked a cow, he also had never seen a live cow, and he wasn't sure he wanted to if it was as big as the mules.

"Come on. You've got a lot to learn, and we might as well get started," Grandpa said, walking toward the open barn door.

Matt followed hesitantly. The sweet fragrance of hay mixed with an acid smell that grew stronger as he approached the far end of the barn.

"Bonnie, you've got a visitor," Grandpa said.

His announcement was greeted with a soft "mmm-ooo-ooo" from the stall at the far end of the barn. Grandpa stepped into the enclosure, at the same time giving Bonnie's wide rump a slap. She moved over, making room for Grandpa to move to the feed trough at the back of the stall.

"Come on 'round but watch where you step. We'll have to clean out the stall this morning after I turn Bonnie out to pasture."

Matt heard the "we'll" as he stepped around the pungent dark brown pile on the straw covered dirt floor. He flattened himself against the side of the stall trying to stay as far away from the cow as he could. She was so big he could just see over the top of her back. Bonnie turned her head and looked at him with long-lashed brown eyes. Stray pieces of hay stuck out the sides of her mouth as she chewed. She flipped her tail to chase away an annoying fly and then ignored Matt.

"What happened to her horns?" asked Matt.

"Some have'm, some don't," said Grandpa, as though any right-thinking person would know.

Grandpa gave Bonnie a little shove. She backed out of the stall, turned, and headed out the back door of the barn and down the well-worn path that led into the pasture.

Grandpa walked over to where tools were hanging on the wall. Taking down two pitchforks, he handed one to Matt.

"Let's get Bonnie's stall mucked out. It's better to do it before the heat sets in."

He brought a wheelbarrow to the stall and began loading it with the fouled hay. As he moved the hay, the smell was stronger. Matt thought he was going to be sick.

Grandpa looked over his shoulder at Matt.

"Come on, boy! Don't just stand there. Lend a hand."

Matt stepped forward and pushed his pitchfork into the hay. He tried not to breath as he lifted the hay to the wheelbarrow.

When the wheelbarrow was full, Grandpa pushed it to a small wagon just outside the back door of the barn.

"Fork some of that clean hay into the stall," said Grandpa as he pushed back his straw hat and wiped his brow on his sleeve.

Matt heard the roar of an engine as he finished pitching hay in the stall. Looking out the barn door, he saw Grandpa hooking a John Deere tractor to the wagon that was piled high with fouled hay from the barn.

"Throw the pitchforks in the wagon and hop on," Grandpa said. "Once a week, I empty the wagon in the pasture down by the creek."

Matt climbed on the wagon. He was glad when the tractor started moving, blowing the smell in the other direction.

At the far end of the pasture near the creek, Grandpa stopped the tractor, and they spread the hay on the ground.

"This'll dry out and the critters will eat every bit of it," Grandpa said.

"What critters?" asked Matt.

"Oh, wild hogs, armadillo, and birds. Nothin' ever goes to waste. There are all sorts of things here 'bouts—fox, bobcats, maybe a catamount or bear, and all sorts of snakes. The cottonmouth is over by the creek and the rattler can be just about anywhere. You have to keep your eyes open."

Matt looked around. He had thought all he had to worry about was two dogs!

"Are there any fish in the creek?" asked Matt on the way back to the barn.

"There're crappie, catfish, and bream. They all make good eatin'. The water's still pretty high now, but later in the summer, the creek'll be near dry if we don't get rain," Grandpa said as he pulled the tractor and wagon up to the back of the barn. "But we're bound to get a few big storms before summer's over."

Chapter 4

Everyone piled in the car the next morning to take Matt's mother to catch the train. Lady chased after the car until they were at the end of the long drive. She had tried to get into the car, but Grandma said she had to stay home.

"Matthew did a good job mucking out the stall yesterday," Grandpa said. "Before you know it, he'll be milking Bonnie, gathering the eggs, and plowing the field. We won't have to do anything but sit on the porch in those rocking chairs you're always talking about getting." He looked sideways at Grandma and smiled.

"You shouldn't 'spect too much of the boy," said Grandma, "After all, he wasn't brought up on a farm."

Matt was surprised Grandpa said anything good about the work he'd done.

*　　*　　*

The Cotton Belt was right on time. As the train came to a stop at the station platform, the steam from the engine added humidity to the already hot morning. The windows on the coach were up. Once the train was moving, there would be a breeze to help cool the car.

It was all Matt could do to hold back tears when his mother hugged him goodbye. He felt abandoned when the train pulled away from the station.

"It sure is hot," Grandma said as they turned away from the station platform. "Let's go over to Doc Roberts's and get an ice cream cone or an ice cream soda. What would you like, Matthew?"

"I'd like a chocolate sundae. That's my favorite," Matt said.

"Air Conditioned" read a sign painted on the glass in the front door of the drugstore. The blue lettering was edged in white "icicles."

As Grandpa opened the door for Grandma, a wave of cool air washed over them. It was like stepping from summer into winter. With the cool air came a whiff of *Midnight In Paris* from the perfume counter mixed with the antiseptic smell of a doctor's office from the pharmacy.

"Hello, Mr. Morrison, Mrs. Morrison. Haven't seen you in a while," said a smiling man in a white jacket as he came out of the pharmacy at the back of the store.

"We've stayed well, Doc, and haven't had much call to drop in on you lately," Grandpa said.

"What can I do for you now?"

"We've brought our grandson Matthew in to get your best remedy for a hot day. He's spending the summer with us. Matthew, this here's Doc Roberts."

"Pleased to meet you, sir."

"You look a lot like your dad," Doc said. "It seems like it wasn't long ago when he was coming in for something cool. Most of the time, he'd have a Coke, but when he splurged, he'd have a chocolate sundae."

"That's my favorite too."

"Well, in honor of this occasion, let me treat you."

Matt climbed on one of the tall stools in front of the soda fountain to watch Doc make the sundae.

"Your daddy was the soda jerk here the summer before he joined the army. I think he ate as much ice cream as he sold the first week. He didn't seem too interested in ice cream after that."

Matt still had trouble thinking of his father as a boy. All he could remember was his father, the soldier.

"I was surprised when he joined up. Guess your grandparents were too. I think your grandpa expected him to stay and work the farm. But then, our kids don't always do what we think they will," Doc Roberts commented.

Doc put a cherry on top of the sundae and slid it across the counter to Matt. The whipped cream looked like the snow cap on a mountain of ice cream and chocolate syrup. Should he eat the cherry first or save it for last?

While Matt considered his sundae, Doc Roberts made two ice cream sodas and took them to Matt's grandparents who were sitting in a booth near the back of the store.

Before he could make up his mind about the cherry, the doorbell jangled as two boys sauntered in. Their cowboy boots made a racket as they ambled across the room. The taller one walked with a swagger that the other imitated.

"I think we've got a city boy here, Ray. Just look at those little boy pants," the taller boy said, pointing to Matt's knickers.

Matt could feel his face getting red. His mother had promised to buy long pants for school in the fall.

To make matters worse, the boy looked at Matt's sundae and reached for the cherry. When Doc Roberts walked over, he drew his hand back.

"Good morning, Jake—Ray," he said, nodding to each in turn. "What can I do for you, boys?"

Jake, the boy who had reached for the cherry, gave Matt a mocking look before turning to Doc Roberts.

"Ma sent us in for some headache powders," he said, brushing imaginary dust from the sleeve of his colorful striped western shirt. Both his shirt and the blue-and-white checkered western style shirt his brother wore looked new.

"Those are some fine-looking shirts you boys are wearing," Doc said. "You planning on doing some rodeoing?"

"You might say we are," Jake said. He looked over his shoulder at Ray. "Wouldn't you say we're going to do some rodeoing?"

Both of the boys laughed at a private joke.

As Doc talked with the boy about the powders, Matt slid off the stool, took his sundae, and went to sit in the booth with his grandparents.

Before he took the first bite, he thought about what he could have done to protect his reputation and his sundae. (Mostly, his sundae.) Should he have bitten the offending hand? Maybe knocked the boy down with one mighty blow? No, it was better to have escaped while he could. But when he got older and bigger, nobody, but nobody, was going to mess with him.

With that settled, Matt ate the cherry.

"I believe we need to go to the hardware store," Grandma said when they finished their treats and were on the sidewalk.

"What for?" Grandpa asked.

Matt, walking ahead of them, didn't hear Grandma's reply.

There were double screened doors at the front of the hardware store. Inside, ceiling fans moved at a lazy pace.

"'morning, Oscar, Mrs. Morrison. What can I do for you?" asked the tall man standing behind the counter, looking over the top of his eyeglasses.

"'morning, Emory," Grandpa replied. "You'll have to ask Mrs. Morrison. She's in charge. By the way, this is our grandson Matthew, Sam's son. He's spending the summer with us."

Emory reached out and shook Matt's hand.

"You look a lot like your dad," he said. Much to Matt's relief, he didn't seem to notice the knickers.

The store was different from any Matt had seen. It wasn't just a hardware store. There was a small section with dishes and pots and pans. Another with furniture and another with clothes.

"Emory, we're looking for some overalls for Matthew. And a shirt or two," said Grandma as she led the way to the back of the store.

Emory pointed to a table of neatly folded overalls. Matt started to protest. He had never worn overalls. None of his friends wore overalls.

"Grandma, couldn't I have a pair of long pants?" Matt asked.

"Right now, you need overalls, Matthew. You'll find that's what most of the boys around here wear. You're at an age where you're growing, so we'll buy them a little large."

Matt's heart sank. Not only would he not get long pants, he would also be wearing overalls that were too big.

"If they're too long, you can just roll 'em up," Grandpa said. "If they get too short, you can let out the shoulder straps. They'll be just fine."

They left the hardware store with two pairs of blue denim overalls and two long-sleeved light blue cotton shirts.

"Those overalls cost almost as much as mine," grumbled Grandpa when they were on their way back to the house.

"A dollar and a quarter apiece is a lot to pay. At least the shirts were on sale. And on top of that, you had to use some of our rationing stamps."

"If you're expecting Matthew to do more than gather eggs, he has to have some proper clothes," Grandma said.

"Harump!" was Grandpa's reply.

"Speaking of shirts, did you notice the fancy shirts the Wilson boys were wearing?" Grandma asked Grandpa. "Those certainly didn't come from Emory's. I can't imagine how their mother could afford them."

Chapter 5

When Grandpa knocked on the bedroom door the next morning, Matt realized he would be expected to help with the chores every day. As far as he was concerned, summer was for playing, but on the farm, it seemed everybody worked all the time.

As he dressed in his new overalls, he could hear bits of his grandparents' conversation in the next room.

"...and his vacation has just started...let him sleep late," Grandma said.

"...just like his daddy. Chores need to be done...no need in him sitting around...." Grandpa replied.

"...thought he was a man, but he wasn't quite man enough," he continued, his voice rising.

"How can you forgive somebody who never says they're sorry?" Grandpa asked.

It embarrassed Matt to overhear what they were saying. What had Grandpa meant by "How can you forgive somebody who never says they're sorry?" Who had never said they were sorry, and for what?

When he settled into his chair at the breakfast table, he noticed a frown on Grandpa's face. Grandma looked sad as she turned from the stove to put a plate of biscuits on the table. She brightened and smiled as she said "good morning" to him and gave him a hug. It seemed the hug was as much to make her feel better as it was to show affection to Matt.

After an awkward silence, Grandpa got up from the table and started for the back door.

"When you've finished breakfast, Matthew, make yourself useful. There're chores to be done," he said.

Grandma put a plate of eggs and bacon in front of Matt, fixed herself a cup of coffee, and sat down at the table.

"Why is Grandpa so grumpy?" asked Matt. "Most of the time he acts like he doesn't like me."

Grandma sat looking into her coffee cup as though she might find the answer there.

"Your grandpa's a good man. He's worked hard all his life and had more than his share of disappointments. One of his greatest disappointments was your daddy wouldn't stay to work the farm with him. The two of them were always arguing.

"When your daddy finished high school, he was restless and looking for something to do besides farm. A lot of men were out of work then, so there weren't many jobs around here. One day, he came home from town and told us he had joined the army. It was before America was at war."

"Well, he and your grandpa argued most of the night. In the morning, your daddy left before we got up. He came home after basic training, but he and your grandpa have never really settled their differences. They're both stubborn and too proud for their own good," Grandma said.

Matt ate his breakfast in silence. He thought grown-ups had it a lot easier than kids. After all, if you're a grown-up, you get to make all the decisions, and because you're a grown-up, you're always right. Or at least that's the way he had thought it went.

With breakfast over, Matt helped Grandma clear the table. He put off going outside as long as he could.

"Can I help you feed the chickens and gather the eggs?" Matt asked. He was sure taking care of the chickens would be better than working in the barn or doing whatever Grandpa had planned for him.

"That'll be a big help. I'll come out with you and show you what to do as soon as I finish washing these dishes."

Matt didn't wait for Grandma. He didn't need to be shown. How hard could it be to gather some eggs and throw some corn on the ground?

He picked up the egg basket from the chair beside the back door and followed the well-worn path around the corner of the barn to the fenced chicken yard. The chickens were quietly scratching in the dirt in the enclosure.

A rooster stood in the far corner. His black tail feathers gave off an iridescent shimmer. He stood tall, stretched out his neck, opened his wings wide, and crowed. He flapped his wings a few times and looked around as if to make sure everyone noticed him.

Matt opened the wire gate. The rooster turned his head and watched closely. When Matt was halfway across the yard, the rooster, his head jutting forward and wings outstretched, raced toward Matt. A mad dash to the hen house gave Matt just enough time to slip through the door and slam it before the rooster caught him. Who would have thought a bird could run so fast?

Matt looked through the cracks between the boards in the door. The rooster was standing in front of the hen house with his head tilted to one side and his beady little eyes fixed on the door. He wasn't going to move.

Matt looked around to see if there was another way out of the small building. There wasn't. A dozen straw-lined boxes were nailed to a sidewall. Wooden racks for roosting filled the back wall. *I'll bet today is the day the hen house is supposed to be cleaned*, Matt thought as he tried not to breathe too deeply. The smell was awful.

"Matthew. Matthew. Are you in the hen house?"

He pressed his eye to the crack in the door. Grandma was standing outside the fence, looking around.

The rooster hadn't moved.

"I'm in here, Grandma," replied Matt. "That rooster chased me."

"Roscoe can be a problem if you don't know how to handle him," said Grandma as she opened the gate and stepped into the yard.

Duke and Lady had heard the commotion and were sitting by the fence, watching. Matt knew dogs couldn't laugh, but they certainly looked like they were enjoying the proceedings. Duke's long ears flopped as he shook his head from side to side. Lady gave one bark in agreement before a flea caught her attention.

Grandma picked up the basket Matt had dropped and walked calmly toward Roscoe. She waved her apron at him a few times, and he retreated to the other side of the chicken yard.

Matt opened the door, and Grandma handed him the basket.

"Sometimes things that seem easy to do aren't," Grandma said, "especially on a farm. There's no shame in asking questions or asking for advice. Just remember that, and you'll save yourself a lot of grief."

"Yes, 'um," Matt said. He was glad Grandma had come to his rescue and not Grandpa.

Matt was right about this being the day to clean the hen house. After the eggs were gathered and the chickens fed and watered, Grandma sent him to the barn for a rake, a shovel, and a bucket. Matt raked the dirt floor of the hen house and shoveled droppings into the bucket.

"You can empty that on the ground by the side of the house. I'm going to put in a fall garden there. If we work the soil and fertilize it now, it'll be in fine shape when it's time to plant," Grandma said as she and Matt walked to the garden site.

It took Matt most of the morning to clean out the hen house. He was in no rush to finish. There was no telling what Grandpa might want him to do.

He stopped three times to go to the kitchen where Grandma had put a pitcher of lemonade on the table. Then he had to stop three times to go to the bathroom. He put only a couple of shovels full of droppings into the bucket for each trip to the garden site. All the while, Duke and Lady followed, keeping watch on what he was doing and where he was going.

"Don't you have anything better to do?" he asked the dogs as he made his fourth trip to the garden site. They never came very close, and he was beginning to get used to them. As he was leaning the shovel against the barn, a bell began to ring. Matt looked and saw Grandma was standing on the back porch, ringing the large bell that hung under the eaves.

"What's wrong, Grandma?" Matt called out as he ran toward the house.

"Nothing's wrong. I'm ringing the bell so Grandpa will know to come in for dinner," said Grandma.

It was funny to call the noon meal dinner. At home, he and his mother had lunch at noon and dinner at night. Now he had supper at night.

When they sat down at the table, Matt could see why this was called dinner. A large platter of fried chicken was in the middle of the table. It was surrounded by bowls filled with green beans and potato salad and platters of corn on the cob and sliced tomatoes. The ever-present basket of biscuits was on one corner of the table. A bowl of sliced peaches sat ready to be spooned into dessert dishes. Tall glasses of sweet iced tea stood at each place.

Grandpa asked the blessing and began passing the food. Matt filled his plate. He hadn't realized how hungry he was until he sat down at the table.

"Matthew gathered the eggs this morning and cleaned out the hen house," Grandma said as she passed the biscuits to Grandpa.

"That's good," said Grandpa, "but he forgot to clean the shovel and bucket. And he didn't put them away when he finished—left them outside the barn. Matthew, be sure you take care of that after dinner."

"Yes, sir." He might have known Grandpa would notice what he hadn't done.

Matt helped Grandma clear the table after dinner and then started for the back door.

"Matthew, if you're going to be spending time outside, you're going to be needing a hat. Look in your daddy's closet and see if one's on the top shelf," Grandma said. "I'm going to write your daddy a letter this afternoon. I haven't heard from him in a while, but I know when you're fighting a war, you don't have much time for letter writing. Do you ever write him?"

"I usually write a little at the end of Mama's letters."

"I'm sure he'd like to hear from you. You could tell him about all you're doing this summer."

"Yes, 'um," Matt said as he went into the bedroom.

He had never written a whole letter. It was hard enough to think of what to say when he wrote a few lines at the end of his mother's letters. He might give it a try. He'd think about it.

Chapter 6

On the top shelf of the closet were two cowboy hats. One was a dark-brown felt with a low crown and the other was a straw with a high crown. Matt took them into the kitchen.

"These were in the closet," he said as he held them out for Grandma to see.

"Yes, those are the ones I remember. The brown one is for winter, and the straw for summer. Try on the straw and let's see how it fits."

The hat was a little big, but he liked it.

"Would it be all right if I wear one of the bandanas too?"

"Certainly. I'm sure your daddy would like that."

As Matt put the felt hat away in the closet, he looked around to see what else was there. On the floor at the back of the closet, he found a small, wooden keg. The top and bottom of the keg had been removed. A taunt piece of leather covered one end. A hole was punched in the leather, and a long thin string of rawhide had been threaded through and knotted on the outside. The rawhide string hung out the open end of the keg.

"Grandma, what is this?" Matt asked as he carried the keg into the kitchen. "It looks like some kind of drum."

"Lawd 'a' mercy," Grandma said as she took the keg from Matt. "I thought your grandpa had thrown that out a long time ago. It caused more trouble than I ever want to think about. Your daddy made it. I don't know where he got the idea."

"If you take hold of the string like this," she said, reaching inside the keg and taking hold of the rawhide with the tips of her fingers, "and pull down on it, it makes an awful noise. It sounds enough like a catamount to fool a body."

"What's a catamount? Grandpa said there are some around here."

"Some people call them pain'ers or cougars, but around here we call 'em catamounts." She pulled her fingertips gently down the string. A deep, resonant screech sounded from the keg. It sent chills up Matt's spine.

"Of course, that wasn't nearly as loud as it can get if you pull down hard. When your daddy took it out to the barnyard to see what the mules would do when they heard it, they panicked, broke through the corral, and stampeded in all directions. It took three days to round up all of them. Now put that thing back where you found it. Don't be playing around with it."

Matt put the keg in the closet. He took a red bandana with a white lightning-bolt design on it from the drawer and stuffed it in his back pocket as he walked out the back door. Pulling the hat down over his eyes the way he had seen movie cowboys do, he looked around.

His mother had always insisted he not leave their block at home by himself. Now he had acres and acres to explore all alone.

It was so quiet. The afternoon heat had settled in. Duke and Lady were sleeping in the shade on the front porch. They couldn't be bothered with exploring. It was nap time.

Matt set out to follow the fence line and see where it took him.

After walking a short distance, he turned off the path and followed a faint trail that led through the woods, grasshoppers flew up from the weeds that brushed against his pants legs. He sat down on the bank of a narrow creek and settled comfortably against a tree trunk. Matt had just given in to the hypnotic sound of the gurgling stream and the buzzing insects when he awoke with a start. Something was thrashing in the underbrush!

The sound was coming toward him. What if it was a wild hog or a catamount? He scrambled to his fee and started to run.

As he crossed a clearing, he looked back. Three animals bounded after him. They looked as though they were wearing knights' armor. The little ones began chasing each other and rolling on the ground.

A fallen tree was the only shelter in sight. Matt threw himself over the trunk and lay still. The animals stopped in the clearing where the big one began rooting around in the leaves.

"Um, um. That weren't very smart. Old Joe No-shoulders could'a been taking his afternoon nap right there."

At the sound of the voice, Matt whirled around.

There was Grandpa's mule Jenny. Sitting casually on her back, with his long, overall-clad legs hanging down to her belly, was the darkest boy Matt had ever seen. Before he could respond, the other boy went on.

"If you're gonna be out here, you needs to know a few things. One is old Joe No-shoulders, you know, rattlers, copperheads, and the likes, takes napes under old logs. Old Joe might get mad and bite you if you wakes him up. Mind, you don't want to meet up with no coachwhip neither. If he don't bite you, he'll wrap hisself 'round you and beat you to death with his tail."

"I was hiding from those wild animals," Matt said defensively, looking around quickly to see what might be lurking under the log. "They've been chasing me all the way from the creek."

The boy pulled up one long leg, rested his foot on Jenny's back and looked at the animals.

"That's a mama armadillo and her pups. Ain't no way she's gon'ta bother you."

"What're you doing on my grandpa's mule?" Matt asked belligerently. He was embarrassed and wanted to change the subject.

"No need to get all het up," the boy said. "I was just on my way home from Mr. Wright's farm when your grandma asked me to find you. She's afraid you'd gone and got yourself lost. Of course, I can tell you ain't lost, and you'd have been home afore long—if the wild animals didn't get you first."

"By the way, I'm Joshua. You know, like Joshua the mighty warrior what made the walls come tumbling down? When I was a baby, I cried so loud my daddy called me Joshua because he thought the walls might fall down any minute. I was really named after my granddaddy John Parker Williams, but everybody calls me Joshua. Not Josh, mind you, Joshua!"

"Oh" was all Matt could think to say. "I'm Matthew Barnwell Morrison. Most people call me Matt."

"Well, Matt, if you'll stand on that log and mount up, we'll be getting back to the house," Joshua said as he guided Jenny over to the log.

Standing on the log didn't make Matt tall enough to mount the mule. Joshua told him to throw himself on his stomach onto Jenny's back, swing his right leg over her rump and sit up. On the second try, Matt managed to land on his stomach with his head hanging off one side and his legs on the other. Jenny started to move as he was struggling to throw his leg over. It was all he could do to stay on.

"Hey, stop! I'm gonna fall off," Matt yelled as he struggled to swing his leg over her rump.

"You're just fine," Joshua said with a chuckle. "I'll have you back at the house in no time."

Matt bounced along hanging over the back of the mule. He kept struggling until he was finally able to swing his leg over and sit up.

"My daddy always sez, 'Every time you do something for yourself, you learns something,'" Joshua said. "Next time you needs to get on Jenny, you'll know how. Now don't that make you feel better?"

Matt wasn't thinking about next time. He was just trying not to fall off this time. And besides, he thought Joshua seemed to have gotten too much fun out of having him bounce along on his stomach.

Riding out of the woods into a clearing filled with rows of small, dead trees, Joshua brought Jenny to a halt. There were piles of charred wood between the rows. The weeds had begun to reclaim what had once been cleared land.

"This used to be your granddaddy's peach orchard. A couple of years ago, a late freeze killed 'em all. Me and my daddy came over to help your granddaddy build fires between the rows to keep the trees from freezin', but it didn't do no good. All the trees froze and split."

Matt looked at the dead trees. This must be one of the disappointments Grandma had mentioned.

Joshua turned Jenny toward the far end of the field where a dirt road led to the house. As they came over a rise, Matt could see the house with Grandpa's truck parked near the barn.

Once they were inside the corral, Matt said sarcastically as he slid from Jenny's back to the ground, "Thanks for giving me a ride back."

"Any time," Joshua replied, taking the bridle off Jenny. He gave her a pat on the rump, and she moved out to join the other mules.

"Thanks for bringing Matthew home," Grandma called from the back door.

"You're welcome, Miz Morrison. I didn't have nothing else to do. It was a good afternoon for a ride," Joshua replied as he stepped outside the corral and closed the gate.

When Matt walked up from the corral, Grandpa was drawing water from the pump on the back porch.

"You'd better wash up before you go in for supper. Grandma won't let you sit down at the supper table if you haven't brushed off your clothes and washed your hands and face," Grandpa said, tossing soapy wash water from the old enamel bowl onto a plant growing by the porch.

Matt bushed off his clothes, drew fresh water into the bowl, and washed as Grandpa instructed. He even emptied the bowl onto the plant. He figured he couldn't go wrong imitating Grandpa.

"Good move, Matthew. Grandma told me to always pour the soapy water on the gardenia. It keeps the bugs off," Grandpa said.

After all that had gone wrong, Matt was glad he had done something right.

"You know, Matthew," Grandpa said, looking around the yard. "I've always wondered what happened to the family treasure that was buried someplace on the farm. We've dug up a lot of ground but never found a thing."

"Grandpa, what treasure are you talking about?" Matt asked as they walked into the kitchen.

"Treasure?" Grandma asked.

"Sure, Bertha, you remember me telling you how our family treasure was buried during the war."

"What war was that?" Matt asked.

"Why, the War Between the States of course," Grandpa said as though there had never been any other.

Grandma laughed. "My grandmother always called it 'The Recent Unpleasantness.' But I didn't know any battles had been fought around here."

"There weren't," said Grandpa. "But toward the end of the war, raiders were all over this part of the country. They didn't care which side you were fighting for. They were nothing but outlaws—raiding towns and farms and taking whatever they could."

"You mean there were outlaws right here?" asked Matt. He stood wide-eyed imagining rough looking men riding into the yard with their guns drawn.

"No, they never came here, but my grandpa was sure they would, so he buried my grandma's silver and jewelry. My pa was still away fighting and Grandpa wouldn't tell anyone where he had buried it. He said only the man of the house should know."

"What happened? Why didn't he dig it up after the war?" asked Matt.

"My grandpa died of pneumonia the winter before my pa came home. He took the secret to the grave with him," said Grandpa with a sigh. "Well, enough about that. Let's enjoy some of your grandma's cooking."

After Grandpa asked a blessing, Grandma put a dishcloth-lined basket filled with golden brown biscuits fresh from the oven on the table. Supper was always leftovers from dinner, but Grandma had a way of making it special.

"Do you think you could find something for dessert?" Grandpa asked Grandma. They both laughed.

"You know, Matthew, your grandma has served dessert every night since we got married. But I always ask, just to check and make sure."

Tonight, the dessert was butterscotch pie with pecans around the edge. After eating a big slice, Matt gave a contented sigh. Then he asked, "Grandpa, do you think I could dig for the treasure?"

"You're welcome to, but I don't think you'll find anything," Grandpa said. "Oh, by the way, when I was over at the feed store in Mt. Pleasant this afternoon, there was talk of some rustling going on. Seems like a few people have lost a head or two of cattle. Matthew, when you're out and about, keep your eyes peeled for any unusual goin's on."

"Yes, sir," Matt said. "Do you mean real rustlers like in the movies?"

Matt envisioned the cowboys and rustlers in a running gun battle as they fought for the cattle.

"I don't know how they do it in the movies," said Grandpa, "but whoever is doing this is loading one or two head into a truck and driving off with them."

Matt was disappointed. Who ever heard of a rustler in a truck? Rustlers were supposed to be on horseback and wear black ten-gallon hats.

That night, Matt sat at the kitchen table and wrote a letter to his father. He didn't know quite what to say, but once he began putting words on paper, he found it wasn't too difficult.

Dear Daddy,

I'm spending the summer with Grandma and Grandpa on the farm because Momma is afraid I'll catch polio if I stay in the city. I don't want to catch polio, but I didn't want to come here either. When I first got to the farm, I thought there wouldn't be anything to do because there aren't many people around. But since I've been here a few days, I'm beginning to like it. I rode a mule with Joshua this afternoon. He's the first colored person I've ever talked to. Have you ever talked with any colored people? Grandpa told us after supper tonight that there are rustlers stealing horses and cattle and putting them in a truck. It's time for me to go to bed now.

Love, your son Matt

There, that was easier than he had thought it would be. Maybe he'd do it again.

Chapter 7

The next morning, as Matt dressed, he wondered what chores Grandpa would want him to do today. He decided he might be able to avoid the ones he didn't want to do if he volunteered to dig the garden for Grandma. Having settled that in his mind, he joined his grandparents in the kitchen.

"Grandma," he said, "I thought I'd start digging that garden this morning if that's all right with you."

He turned to Grandpa. "That is if you don't have something more important for me to do."

Grandpa looked at him. "No, I guess there isn't anything more important than digging your grandma's garden," he replied.

Matt could tell by the look on Grandpa's face that he hadn't fooled him.

As Grandpa showed him how to turn the dirt over and how deep to dig, Grandma came out and watched for a few minutes.

"It'll be wonderful to have a winter vegetable garden so close to the house," Grandma said. "Having an extra pair of hands on a farm makes a big difference."

"Yes, 'um," he mumbled. He wondered what she would think if she knew he was doing this just to get out of whatever chore Grandpa had planned for him.

A little while later, he wasn't sure he had been so smart. The dirt was heavier and harder to turn than he had thought it would be. He was wearing a pair of gloves Grandpa had given him, but he could feel blisters beginning to form. The hat offered a little shade, but sweat was running down his face.

"Mornin'," came a cheerful greeting from behind him.

He turned around to find Joshua standing with his arms folded across his chest, his head cocked to one side and that big grin on his face.

"Seems like they got you workin' already this mornin'," Joshua said.

Matt stopped digging, leaned on his shovel, and wiped his brow with the big red bandana.

"I'm not working," Matt said. "I'm digging for treasure."

"Treasure?" Joshua asked. "What treasure?"

"Oh, my great-granddaddy buried a treasure, and I'm going to dig it up."

"Are you sure?"

"Of course, I'm sure. You don't think I'd be out here digging in the hot sun if it weren't for something important like treasure, do you?"

"No, I guess not. But you're not digging very deep. How do you expect to find treasure if you don't dig down deep?"

"Well, you see, it's like this. My great-granddaddy didn't have time to dig very deep because the raiders were coming."

"What raiders?" Joshua asked.

"Outlaws—really bad men who were pillaging and burning," Matt said, warming to the telling of the tale. He thought adding "pillaging" gave the story a special ring. He had read about it in his history book.

Joshua was impressed with Matt's explanation. He wasn't sure what pillaging was, but he wasn't going to ask.

"You know, Grandpa said that anybody who finds the treasure will get a reward," Matt said. He kept his eyes on the ground and continued digging.

"He did?" exclaimed Joshua. "Where can I find me a shovel?"

"There're some hanging on the wall inside the barn. Help yourself."

With Joshua's efforts added, Matt could see real progress being made.

When Grandma came out of the house with glasses of iced water for them, he was afraid she would say something that would give away his scheme.

"Joshua, it sure is nice of you to help Matthew. When you get ready to go home, stop by the kitchen, and I'll give you some eggs to take home to your momma."

"Yes 'um, Miz Morrison. I'll sure do that. Momma said to tell you the can'lope is coming in soon, and she'll send some over."

"That'll be nice," Grandma said.

Matt relaxed when she went back in the house and left the boys to their work.

Grandpa came out of the fields when Grandma rang the dinner bell. As he approached the boys, he called out, "How's that garden coming?"

"Garden?" exclaimed Joshua as he turned to Matt.

Matt cringed, not knowing what would happen next. Maybe fooling Joshua hadn't been such a good idea after all.

Joshua stood, his head cocked to one side and his arms folded across his chest, looking at Matt for what seemed like hours. Then he burst out laughing.

"I guess we can call it even," he said. "But I think you got the better end of the deal. You had to ride a mule on your belly for only a few minutes. I spent most of the morning diggin' in the hot sun."

"We might have found something," Matt said defensively. "Grandpa, didn't you tell me last night that your grandpa had buried treasure someplace on the farm?"

"We've always called it the family treasure, but I doubt that it was much. You have to remember they weren't rich folks—just ordinary farmers like us. They might have buried a box with a few pieces of silver flatware they'd brought with them from Tennessee and maybe a locket or two. You won't be finding a chest full of gold."

"I think I've done enough treasure diggin'," Joshua said. "I'll be on my way."

"Now don't be mad."

"I told you we're even. I just ain't doing your chores for you."
Joshua turned and walked away.

Chapter 8

After dinner, Matt stood on the front porch trying to decide where he would explore next. He started down the road that led past the remains of the peach orchard. Just beyond the orchard was a field covering what Matt thought would be three or four city blocks. Lush green vines were growing in every direction, and resting among the leaves were watermelons.

Matt had never seen such a sight. Just looking at all those melons made his mouth water. They were a rare treat at his house. He always looked forward to the Fourth of July picnic because he knew he'd get a slice of cold, sweet watermelon.

Standing at the edge of the field, he began to count the melons. He stopped when he got to fifteen. There must be hundreds of them—maybe even thousands—way out here in the middle of nowhere—all by themselves.

Matt walked down the road beside the field. He couldn't take his eyes off the long, striped, green melons. He could just imagine the sweet red insides dotted with black seeds. The more he looked, the slower he walked. He stopped beside a melon that was growing a little closer to the road than the others.

Should he pick it up and put it back in the field? He lifted it and moved it away from the road. Maybe that wasn't the right place to put it. As he picked it up again, he stepped on the vine…accidentally. The vine broke.

Matt stood at the edge of the field holding the watermelon. Should he put it down and leave it there? It would be wasted if he just left it. No, now that it was picked, it had to be eaten. That would be up to him.

Carrying the melon past the orchard and down the path he and Joshua had followed, he made himself comfortable in the shade by the creek. As he pulled out his pocketknife, he heard someone coming. He looked for a place to hide the melon, but he wasn't fast enough.

There was Joshua with a fishing pole over his shoulder.

"Whatcha got there?" Joshua asked.

Matt didn't know just exactly what to say.

"Your grandpa don't grow no melons. Where'd you get that?"

"From that field over yonder. No, not from the field. You see, that was the problem. The melon was growing too close the road. When I tried to pick it up and move it over, I accidentally stepped on the vine and broke it. I couldn't just leave it there in the hot sun."

"Um, um, that sounds like a real problem. So you is bringin' the melon to the creek to cool it off? You ain't thinking of eatin' it all by yo'self is you? Cause I'd be more 'n happy to help you."

"Well, I guess I could use some help."

Matt was beginning to feel uneasy about having taken the watermelon. If he gave Joshua some, maybe he wouldn't tell anybody.

"Tell ya what, you put the melon in the creek to cool off, and I'll catch us some fish. We'll have some fine eatin' 'fore you knows it," Joshua said.

He took a small box from his overalls pocket. Matt stared as Joshua took a cricket from the box and pushed a hook through it.

"If ya gonna catch fish, ya gotta have bait," Joshua said in response to the look of disgust on Matt's face.

"I guess, but I sure wouldn't want to be the bait."

Matt took off his shoes and socks, rolled up his overalls, waded into the creek and gently lowered the watermelon into the cool water. He stood for a moment, watching the dark water flow around his ankles.

"Why's the water so brown? Can you drink it?"

"My daddy says it's brown cause of all the trees growin' along the edge of the water. Once when me and Daddy went squirrel huntin', we camped by the creek and used creek water to drink and make our coffee. The next morning, when we went on upstream, we found a dead cow in the creek," Joshua replied.

Matt couldn't tell whether Joshua was joking or not. He turned and looked upstream. The shallow ribbon of water looked tranquil—no bodies in sight.

"Wish it was deep enough for us to go swimming," he said.

"There's some spots a few miles on deep enough for swimmin', but ya gotta keep an eye out for snakes and snappers," Joshua replied.

"Snappers?"

"Snappin' turtles. Some peoples calls them alligator snappin' turtles. They's mean critters. If they bites ya, they won't let go. You can lose a finger or worse swimmin' with one of them."

Matt quickly waded out of the water. Between dead cows and snapping turtles, the creek had lost some of its appeal.

Joshua flipped his fishing line into the stream. Before long, he had caught five small bream. He showed Matt how to scale and gut the fish with the knife he wore in a leather case at his waist.

"We can cook 'em right here and have the melon for dessert," Joshua said. "We'll dig a pit for the fire close to the creek. That way we won't be startin' no woods fires."

Joshua gathered a few dry sticks and leaves, put them in the pit, and lit them with matches he took from his pocket. He cut sticks, ran them through the fish, and held them over the fire.

Matt thought he had never smelled anything so good. He'd had dinner not two hours before, but suddenly, he was hungry. They ate the fish right off the sticks. Even without salt, they tasted great.

"Throw some creek water on the fire, spread out the ashes, and cover the hole with dirt," instructed Joshua. "Then let's see how good that melon is you rescued from Mr. Wright's patch."

"Who made you boss?"

"Well, I did the catchin' and the cookin'. You gets to do the clean-up. My daddy always sez..."

"Never mind what your daddy always says," retorted Matt.

Joshua just laughed.

After he put out the fire and covered the pit, Matt waded into the creek and picked up the watermelon. Its skin was cool and slippery, making it hard to hold on to.

As Joshua plunged the knife into the melon, it began to split ahead of the blade and juice ran onto the ground.

"O-o-o-e, this here's a real ripe one," Joshua said as he finished cutting the melon in two and pushed half of it toward Matt.

Matt had never seen such a melon. Shiny black seeds surrounded the big red heart of the fruit. It was almost too perfect to eat. Almost.

"Since you brought dessert, you take the first piece," said Joshua as he handed Matt the knife.

Matt cut a piece from the heart of the melon and shoved the cool, sweet, juicy bite in his mouth. He closed his eyes and sighed.

"I've never tasted anything so good in all my life."

He and Joshua sat in silence eating to their hearts' content. Just about the time their stomachs were too full to hold any more, they ran out of watermelon.

"Nobody can say we wasted any of that melon," Joshua said as he lay back against a tree.

Matt hoped he and Joshua would be the only people who would know about the watermelon. He didn't want to think about what would happen if Grandpa found out.

Matt lay back on the leaves, cradling his head in his hands.

"What's on the other side of the creek?"

"Not much. Some creekers used to live in a cabin a little ways over yonder," Joshua said, pointing upstream. "When Daddy and me went huntin', we stayed away from that part of the woods. Daddy says they ain't the kind of folks you wants to meet up with."

"Let's look around and see if we can find where they used to live. We can be explorers like Stanley and Livingston," Matt said.

"Who is Stanley and Livingston?" Joshua asked.

"They were two guys who went exploring in Africa. Stanley thought Livingston was lost, but he wasn't. People just didn't know where he was. When Stanley found Livingston with a native tribe, he walked up and said, 'Dr. Livingston, I presume.' That's how the English talk. John Wayne wouldn't have said anything like that."

Joshua laughed.

"No, sir, he wouldn't have."

"Let's go see if we can find the creekers' cabin," Matt said.

Joshua was reluctant but finally gave in.

They walked upstream to a spot where Joshua pointed out a trail on the other side of the creek.

"I think that's the way to the cabin."

They forded the creek and followed the overgrown trail into the underbrush. After a few minutes, they came into a clearing. On the far side was a dilapidated house with a small outbuilding behind it.

The boys skirted the clearing and the house. It looked deserted and forlorn. Beside the outbuilding was a corral made of saplings.

"Let's see what's inside," Matt said as he walked up the steps to the porch.

He peered through the window into a small dark room. There were only a few pieces of furniture in sight.

"Come on. Let's go," Joshua said, looking over his shoulder. "I don't like the feel of this place."

"Don't be a scaredy-cat. Look, the door isn't locked," Matt said, pushing it open and walking in.

The house had three small rooms. All of them were sparsely furnished. In the kitchen was a table with an oil lamp in the middle of it. The open cupboard held some canned goods.

"Looks like somebody's been here," Matt called to Joshua.

Joshua didn't reply.

"What're ya doin' here, boy?"

Matt turned to see a man standing in the doorway. He was tall, lean, and hard-looking. His green checkered shirt was dirty and stained with sweat. He wasn't smiling—and he was holding a rifle.

"W-w-w-e were just looking around. We didn't know anybody lived here."

"Wha'cha mean 'we'? Is that you and the mouse you got in your pocket? I don't see nobody else around."

Matt looked beyond the man. Joshua had vanished.

"Oh, I mean me and my friends. They're back down by the creek. I just came over to look at the cabin. It's a right nice cabin you have here."

The man didn't say anything but kept glaring at Matt. Finally, he stepped away from the door.

"Get out of here and don't you come back. This is private property."

"Yes, sir, I sure will, I mean, I won't."

Jumping off the porch, Matt dashed for the woods. He didn't slow down until he reached the creek.

"Why didn't you tell me somebody was coming?" Matt yelled at Joshua when he found him crouching behind a tree.

"I heard him just in time to duck out. I figured he most likely wouldn't hurt you. If he'd gotten mean, I could'a run for help."

"A lot of good that would have done. By the time you got back with help, he could have buried my body in the woods!"

"I told you not to go in that shack. I had a bad feeling, but you just wouldn't listen. My daddy sez you should always pay attention to your feelings. They'll keep you out of a lot of trouble."

At the supper table that evening, Matt was still thinking about his encounter at the cabin.

"Grandpa, I was walking by the creek this afternoon and saw a shack on the other side. There was a man there. It's awfully far back in the woods. How do people get back there?"

"That must have been the old creekers' cabin you saw. I didn't know anybody was living there now. There's a dirt road that comes in from the other side, but I don't think it's been used for a long time. Those creekers are a pretty rough lot. The kind of people it's best to stay away from. Don't you be going over there."

Matt didn't eat much supper. He was still full from the fish and watermelon. When Grandma put a big slice of melon in front of him for dessert, he almost groaned out loud.

"This afternoon, Mr. Wright left this melon. He's just beginning to pick them. I knew you'd enjoy a big piece. I'm sure you don't get melons like this in the city," she said.

Matt smiled weakly.

"No, ma'am," he said as he cut a small piece.

When Matt went to bed that night, he felt as though his stomach would explode. He hadn't dared tell Grandma he had eaten half a watermelon that afternoon. He remembered a Bible verse he had learned in Sunday school. It was something about "Your sins will find you out." He wondered if that included taking a watermelon from Mr. Wright's field. And on top of everything else, somewhere along the way, he had lost his daddy's red bandana.

Chapter 9

Next morning, Matt stayed in bed until Roscoe crowed and the sun appeared on the horizon. He could hear the murmur of his grandparents' voices coming from the kitchen.

"I think summer has really set in. It's gettin' hotter and dryer every day," Grandma said by way of greeting when Matt ambled into the kitchen. She stepped away from the stove where breakfast was cooking and wiped her face with her apron.

"I'll get the 'lectric fans out of the shed and clean them up this morning before I do anything else," Grandpa said.

After breakfast, Matt looked through the screened door to where Duke and Lady were waiting on the porch. They seemed to think it was their duty to accompany him when he went to gather the eggs. He wondered if they went to the chicken yard with him just to see if Roscoe would chase him again. Currently, he and the rooster had a truce, but he didn't know how long it would last.

Matt had almost reached the chicken yard when Duke and Lady began to bark and run toward the front of the house. He left the egg basket on the ground and hurried to see what all the commotion was about.

Grandma had heard the dogs and had come out on the front porch.

A large white car pulled up in the drive. Two tall, lean, men wearing khaki western-cut pants, white shirts, and straw Stetsons stepped from the car. Matt stopped when he saw the badges on their chests. One of the men took off his hat as he spoke to Grandma.

Grandma said, "Matt, go tell your grandpa the Texas Rangers want to see him. Be sure you come back with him."

For a minute, Matt couldn't move or speak. Texas Rangers! Were they here about the watermelon? Had Joshua told somebody? Had somebody seen him with the melon? Who would have thought Texas Rangers would come after him for taking one watermelon?

Grandpa was coming out of the storage shed with an electric fan in his hand when Matt found him.

"Aren't you supposed to be gathering eggs for your grandma?"

"Yes, sir, I am. Grandma sent me to tell you there's some Texas Rangers 'round front asking for you."

"Did they say what they wanted?" Grandpa asked, looking puzzled as he put the fan down and started toward the front.

"They talked to Grandma," Matt replied.

Then he took a deep breath and asked, "Grandpa, do they hang people in Texas for taking watermelons?"

Grandpa stopped and turned around. He looked at Matt for a moment before answering.

"They do hang people in Texas, but I haven't heard of anybody gettin' hanged for stealing watermelons—lately. Let's see what the Rangers want, and then we'll talk about watermelon."

Matt didn't realize he was holding his breath until he began to feel lightheaded. He let out his breath and breathed deeply before following Grandpa to where the Rangers were waiting.

After introducing themselves, the Rangers told Grandpa that rustling in the area was becoming a big problem.

"When it first started," said Ranger Stewart, "it just seemed to be amateurs, and the local authorities thought they could take care of it. But lately, we think some professionals have come in with them. That's why we're here from Austin. We understand you have some fine mules. You'll want to be keeping an eye out for strangers in the area who might be interested in them."

"I'd heard some rumors. I'll keep a watch out for anything unusual going on. I sure don't want to lose any of my mules. Thanks for stopping by," Grandpa said.

After the Rangers had gone, Grandma smiled at Matt and said, "I knew you'd want to see some real Texas Rangers. You'll have quite a story to tell your friends when you get home."

"Yes, ma'am," Matt said.

He had thought he might be leaving in the back of the Ranger's car on his way to jail or worse. As it was, he would have to explain everything to Grandpa. That might be just as bad. Matt reluctantly followed Grandpa into the barn.

"Now, what's this about a watermelon?" asked Grandpa.

"Well," said Matt as he tried to decide exactly how much he should tell Grandpa. "I didn't set out to take a watermelon. It was sort of like an accident."

He took a deep breath and went on to tell Grandpa how the watermelon was too close to the road and how he had tried to move it over so it would be safe and how he had accidentally stepped on the vine and broken it. When Grandpa didn't say anything, Matt continued.

"I knew the melon would spoil if I left it there, so I took it to the creek and cooled it off and ate it."

He didn't say anything about Joshua's part in the afternoon's escapade. He didn't say anything about going on the other side of the creek either. He didn't want to get into any more trouble than he was in already.

Matt shifted from one foot to the other as his grandfather walked to the door of the barn, took his hat off, and wiped his forehead with the bandana he pulled from his pocket. He turned and came to stand in front of Matt.

"You've shamed your grandma and me by taking that melon. You might think it's all right to do things like that, but it's not. If your mama and daddy haven't taught you better, it's time somebody did!

"Now, I'll tell you what you're going to do. You're going over to Mr. Wright's and tell him what happened. Then you're going to tell him you'll help with the watermelon harvest today to repay him for that melon. After that, maybe you'll appreciate the hard work that goes into raising melons."

Matt frowned and scuffed the ground with the toe of his shoe.

"I don't want to pick watermelons. Mama gave me some money. I'll just pay Mr. Wright."

"No, you won't. You'll do as I say. I don't want to hear any more back talk out of you. Next thing you know, you'll be taking a swing at me just like your daddy did. And let me tell you, boy, you'll be picking yourself up off the ground—same as he did."

One look at his face told Matt Grandpa meant every word he said.

"Get on now and gather the eggs for your grandma, and then we'll go," Grandpa said as he turned and strode out of the barn.

*　　*　　*

Matt found the egg basket where he left it. As he went through the gate to the chicken yard, Roscoe stretched his neck, flapped his wings, and began his stiff-legged run.

Matt let out a yell, threw his arms in the air, and ran toward Roscoe. One look at Matt and the rooster stopped in his tracks, wheeled around, and raced to the other end of the yard. The hens scattered, and Roscoe and Matt were left facing each other in a gunfighter's standoff.

"If you ever try to chase me again, I'll wring your scrawny neck and eat you for dinner," Matt yelled.

Duke and Lady were on the other side of the fence jumping up and down, barking and wagging their tails. Matt couldn't be sure just who they were cheering for, but he decided they were on his side.

When he took the eggs to Grandma, she said, "Your grandpa told me about the watermelon. Matt, I'm really disappointed in you."

"I'm sorry, Grandma. I didn't start out to take a melon. It sort of happened by accident. I guess I didn't think about it being stealing—there are so many melons in that field. It was like that was just an extra one."

Having Grandma disappointed in him was worse than having Grandpa mad at him. It seemed like Grandpa was mad at him most of the time anyway.

"Well, I hope you've learned your lesson. Grandpa said you'll be going over to Mr. Wright's to help load the watermelons. Here are some ham sandwiches and an apple you can take with you," she said, handing him a paper sack. "You can eat lunch with the other boys."

She said "other boys." Had other boys been stealing melons?

He hesitated at the door.

"Grandma, Grandpa said he and Daddy had a fight, a real fight."

"Yes, they did, I'm sorry to say. It was the night your daddy left. Grandpa told him that as long as he lived under our roof, he'd do as he was told. Your daddy said he would do as he pleased, and Grandpa couldn't stop him. He took a swing at your grandpa. That wasn't very smart of him, but people do dumb things when they're angry."

Chapter 10

Grandpa sat waiting in the wagon behind John Henry and Jenny when Matt came out the back door.

"Climb on up, and we'll get over to the Wright's. I promised to have the team and wagon over earlier, but with the Rangers' visit and other things, I'm a little behind schedule."

As they approached Mr. Wright's field, Matt saw a group of boys about his age loading a wagon with melons. While some were cutting the fruit from the vine, others took the melons to the wagon and handed them up to the crew who put them in the hay that had been spread out on the wagon bed.

"Grandpa, did all those boys take melons?" asked Matt.

"I don't believe so. They're earning money to help buy clothes for school and maybe put a little spending money in their pockets."

As Grandpa pulled up under the trees near the field, a stocky man in overalls walked over to the wagon.

"Morning, Jim," Grandpa said. "Sorry I'm late, but two Rangers stopped by to tell me about the rustlin' going on. Told me I need to keep an eye on my mules."

"'morning, Oscar. I heard Mr. Paulson lost a few head of cattle the other night. Takes nerve to go on his ranch. Must be some pretty slick fellows doing the rustlin'," Mr. Wright replied.

"Must be," Grandpa said, nodding his head in agreement.

"Jim, this is my grandson, Matthew. He's spending the summer with us. He has something he needs to talk about with you."

"Good to meet you, Matthew. What can I do for you?" Mr. Wright asked.

Matt swallowed hard, shifted from foot to foot, wiped his sweaty palms on his overalls, and told Mr. Wright how he had come to take one of his melons. He told Mr. Wright he would be willing to work to make up for taking it.

"I'm sorry I took the melon. I guess I should have brought it to the house and told you what happened. I won't make that mistake again," Matt said as he finished his tale.

He hoped Mr. Wright might not think taking one watermelon was so bad after talking about rustling cattle.

"Matthew, we all have to be careful 'bout the choices we make," Mr. Wright said. "Those rustlers more'n likely started out stealin' some watermelons and moved on up to stealing cattle. One melon won't get you in too much trouble, but stealing cattle will."

"Yes, sir," Matt said. He hoped Mr. Wright didn't think he was planning on stealing any cattle. He didn't want those Rangers coming after him.

"Richard," Mr. Wright called. "Come on over here."

One of the boys in the field stopped what he was doing and walked toward them.

"He'll show you what to do and introduce you to some of the other boys. There's water in the jug at the pump under the tree when you get thirsty. Mrs. Wright will bring out some iced tea when we break for lunch."

"Richard, this here's Matthew, Mr. Morrison's grandson. He's going to be helping us. Introduce him to the rest of the boys."

"Howdy," Richard said. "Glad you've come over to help. We could use another pair of hands."

Matt followed Richard into the field.

"This here's Don, Tob, Jack, Jim, and Charles," Richard said, nodding toward the boys working nearby.

The boys stopped what they were doing and acknowledged the introduction. Matt had met some of them at Sunday school when he went to the Methodist Church with Grandpa and Grandma.

"You ever picked melons before?" Tob asked.

"No," Matt said, "but it doesn't look too hard."

"We'll ask you how you feel 'bout it this evenin'," Jack said.

Jack and Tob were laughing as they moved back into the patch.

The boys on the other side of the field didn't seem to be paying attention to what was going on. Then Matt saw Joshua.

"Hey, Joshua," Matt called and waved.

Joshua looked toward Matt, waved, and went back to work.

"Where do you know him from?" Richard asked.

"We were both fishing in the creek." Matt wasn't going to mention the watermelon. "He showed me how to cook fish on a stick."

"Really? Whenever he's over here workin', he don't seem to have much to say," Richard said. He looked at Matt as though he expected an explanation.

"I guess when he's working, he just doesn't have time to talk," Matt said.

He couldn't imagine Joshua not having something to say. When they were in the woods, he had something to say about everything.

Richard seemed satisfied with Matt's answer. He explained what was going on in the field.

"Some of us are cuttin' the melons off the vines, and some are loadin' them on the wagon. You have to know which melons are ready to cut. Since you don't, you can help carry the melons and load 'em. When a wagon's full, we drive it to Omaha and load the melons into a boxcar on the railroad siding. They'll be going north tomorrow. While the first wagon's gone, we'll be loadin' the second."

"That shouldn't be hard," Matt said.

Richard laughed. "It's not all that easy. You'll see."

By the time Mrs. Wright rang the dinner bell, Matt was dripping with sweat and covered with dirt. His arms and back were so tired he thought he might not be able to move again.

The boys lined up at the pump by the shed and poured the cool water over their heads and wash up before eating. Matt hadn't realized how hungry he was until he bit into one of the thick ham sandwiches from his lunch sack. Before he reached for another sandwich, he washed the first one down with a glass of Mrs. Wright's sweet iced tea.

When they finished eating, they were too tired to horse around. Everyone stretched out under the trees until Mr. Wright rang the bell, signaling it was time to return to the field.

"Matt," called Mr. Wright, later that afternoon. "Hop on the wagon. You can help unload in town."

Joshua, Don, and Jim were already on the wagon when Matt climbed up.

"There's no room for Mr. Wright," said Matt as he looked around.

"Don't need Mr. Wright," Joshua said, picking up the reins. The mules leaned into their harnesses, and the wagon began to move down the road.

"Where'd you learn to drive the team?" Matt asked.

"Your grandpa taught me last summer when my daddy and me was doing some work for him. He said I was a quick learner. I bet he'd teach you if you'd ask."

"I don't think so. He's mad at me."

"How come?"

Matt glanced at the two boys sitting between him and Joshua.

"I'll tell you about it later," he said.

The postman was pulling up to the mailbox when they went by Matt's grandparents' house. He waved to the boys as he put a handful of mail in the box. Matt wondered if he'd ever get a letter from his father.

In town, Joshua brought the mules to a halt beside the open door of a boxcar that had been pulled onto a siding track. There were already watermelons nestled in hay on the floor of the car. Matt and Joshua began unloading the wagon and handing the melons to the other boys who had stepped over into the boxcar.

"Mighty fine mules you got here."

The voice that came from the front of the wagon sounded familiar to Matt.

"These mules belong to Mr. Morrison" came Joshua's reply.

"Whereabouts he lives? I'd like to talk to him about buying them. Maybe we could strike up a deal."

Matt pulled his hat down to shade his face and stepped around from the back of the wagon to get a look at the speaker. The man had been standing in front of the mules looking them over, but when Joshua spoke, he came around to the side. Matt got a good look at him. It was the man from the cabin.

Matt ducked back behind the wagon. He couldn't hear Joshua's reply but hoped he didn't tell the man where the farm was. If the man went and saw Matt, he might tell Grandpa that Matt had been at the cabin. Of course, the man could ask anybody in town where the Morrison place was, and they could tell him. It was just one more thing for Matt to worry about.

The man walked over to a blue pickup truck that was parked in front of the grocery store. The Wilson boys were sitting on the tailgate.

"That man was at the cabin," Matt said as he and Joshua unloaded the watermelons.

"Are you sure?"

"Yeah. He even has on the same shirt. What would he want with mules?"

"Don't know. You gonna tell your grandpa?"

"I don't know. I told him about taking the watermelon. But not about your helping me eat it." Matt hesitated. "He got all mad and said I had shamed the family and said lots of other things. If I tell him about going to the cabin, he might get mad all over again. Joshua, have you ever had a fight with your daddy? I mean a real fight."

"Don't see why I should. Why? Have you?"

"No. The last time I saw him I was only eight. You know, sometimes I feel like he's just somebody I imagined. I've written him two letters since I've been here, but he hasn't written back. I guess when you're fighting a war, you don't have much time for writing."

The boys finished unloading and headed back to the farm. As they drove slowly by the pick-up where the Wilson boys were sitting on the tailgate, Jake Wilson's bright red bandana caught Matt's eye. It looked just like the one he had lost the day he and Joshua had been at the creeker's shack. Was it? And if it was, where had Jake found it? Had he and his brother been at the cabin?

Chapter 11

Quitting time couldn't come soon enough for Matt. This was his fifth day of loading watermelons, and since the second day—the worst—every muscle in his body ached. Grandpa said he had to work only one day to pay for the watermelon, but he went back because he didn't want the other boys to think he was a quitter.

"Okay, boys, come on in," Mr. Wright called. "As y'all know, it's payday." He began to hand out small brown pay envelopes to the workers.

Matt stood behind the rest of the boys. He hadn't hired on to pick the melons. He was there because he had stolen one. To his surprise, Mr. Wright handed him an envelope.

"You're a good worker, Matthew," Mr. Wright said. "Glad you were here to help out this week."

"Gee, thanks, Mr. Wright." Matt couldn't help but grin. He felt at least a foot taller.

Today, Millie and Joe had been pulling the wagon, and Matt imagined they were as glad as he was to be going home. He hadn't counted the money Mr. Wright had given him, but he was already thinking about things he would like to buy.

"Do you know what you're going to do with your money?" Matt asked Joshua, who was again driving the wagon.

"I sure do. I'm saving it for college."

"College? I hadn't even thought about something like that. I'll be in the eighth grade when school starts. College is a long time off, that is, if I go to college."

"Well, I'm going. My mama and daddy didn't finish school. They both had to drop out and get a job when they finished eighth grade. Mama does housework for folks, and Daddy's a carpenter. They wish they could have finished school. It's mighty important to them that I do. And besides, I'm going to be a teacher."

Matt couldn't believe they were having such a conversation. He had been thinking about buying a baseball glove, and here, Joshua was thinking about going to college. He felt a new respect for his soft-spoken, witty friend. Joshua had turned into a different person right before his eyes.

"You know, I believe you'll do it," Matt said as they turned into the barnyard.

*   *   *

"Matthew, you have a letter. I put it on your bed," Grandma said when Matt came in through the kitchen door.

He thought it was most likely from his mother, who had written him every week with news from home.

The envelope had red and blue stripes around the edges and "*V-Mail*" printed on it. The paper was as light and thin as the white tissue paper his mother used to wrap birthday presents. As he carefully opened the letter, Matt's heart beat fast. It had to be from his daddy.

Dear Matt,

> *We've been on the move, and our mail just caught up with us. You can't imagine how glad I was to get mail from your mother and grandmother and three letters from you. We are moving through (here, there was a hole cut in the paper) and don't slow down unless we have to. The Gerries are on the run, and we're chasing them all the way to (another hole).*

Your letters remind me of when I was growing up. To answer your question about colored people, sure I've talked with them and worked with them in the fields and the orchard. Around there, we all depended on each other.

I sure do miss the old home place and the folks. I'd give anything to be able to sit down at the supper table with your mother, your grandparents, and you.

Son, be sure to listen to what your grandpa tells you. You can learn a lot from him.

Love,
Dad

Matt read the letter through two more times, folded it, and carefully put it back in the envelope.

After supper that evening, he went into the front room where Grandpa, bent over, ear pressed against the speaker, was listening to the radio. He waited until Edward R. Murrow's war report from England was over before he spoke.

"Grandpa, I got a letter from my dad today. Wanna read it?"

Grandpa looked surprised. When a frown crossed his face, Matt thought he wasn't going to take the letter.

"I don't think—well, all right."

Grandpa settled his reading glasses on his nose, smoothed the wrinkled letter, and began to read.

His eyes were filled with tears when he finished. He cleared his throat and handed the letter back to Matt.

"That's a nice letter," Grandpa said.

Matt knew that didn't mean everything was patched up between his grandpa and his dad, but he thought it was a start. Maybe he would try to write a letter to his dad all by himself. But what would he write about?

A few days later, Matt had the topic for a letter to his father. Not one he would have picked if he'd had a choice, but one that was sure to hold his father's attention.

He was walking to the creek when he saw an animal lying near the fallen tree in the clearing. At first, he thought it was a dog, but when he got closer, he decided it wasn't.

"What ya got there?" Joshua was standing on the edge of the clearing with his fishing pole over his shoulder. This was the second time he had taken Matt by surprise.

"I don't know," Matt said as he lifted a fluffy tail. "What do you think?"

"Oh, Lordy! That's a fox! Let go that tail. It mighta been mad."

"What difference does it make if it was mad? It's dead now."

"A fox don't just lie down and die like that without something bad wrong with it. It might be a rabid fox," Joshua replied.

Matt laughed.

"You almost had me there for a minute. I guess that rabbit-fox is a cousin of the jackalope Richard was telling me about. He said in West Texas, they have jackalopes—part jackrabbit and part antelope. Even had a picture he tore out of a magazine. There it was, a big rabbit with horns. I might've believed him if Jim hadn't started laughing."

"Nothing to laugh about here. And it's a *rabid* fox—not a *rabbit*-fox. Now, you stay here and, if them dogs show up, keep 'em away from that fox," Joshua said as he started back down the trail.

"Where're you going?" Matt called after him.

"I'm gonna get your grandpa. He'll know what to do."

*   *   *

Grandpa watched as Joshua sprinted across the pasture toward the house.

"What's wrong?" Grandpa yelled.

Joshua didn't answer but kept running to where Grandpa stood by the barn.

"Matt found a dead fox," he said, bending over with his hands on his knees, pausing to catch his breath. "I think it was mad. I seen foam 'round its mouth."

"Good Lord!" Grandpa exclaimed. "Where's Matthew?"

"Left him in the clearing with the fox. It must not have been dead long. No buzzards have showed up yet. I told Matt to keep an eye out for your dogs and make sure they didn't get 'round the carcass."

"Good thinking," Grandpa said. "You get a gunny sack and a pitchfork out of the barn and get in the truck. I'll tell Mrs. Morrison what happened. She can call your mother and let her know."

They were driving through the old peach orchard a short time later.

"I told Mrs. Morrison to call Dr. Smith and tell him we might be in to see him. You know what that means, don't you?"

"Yes, sir," Joshua said. "My cousin Jerimiah got bit by a fox a few years ago. I remember he had to get shots."

"Well, let's not tell Matthew about that. We might be lucky. That fox might have died of old age—but I doubt it."

Chapter 12

Matt was beginning to think Joshua couldn't find Grandpa when the truck pulled into the clearing. He had been sitting on the ground for what seemed like forever holding Duke and Lady by their collars. The dogs barked and struggled to pull loose, but Matt held on.

"Matthew," Grandpa said as he got out of the truck, "you and Joshua put the dogs in the truck cab. When I get this fox in the gunnysack, we'll take it in to be checked for rabies."

Matt thought Grandpa would ask if he was okay, but he didn't.

"Did the dogs get to the fox?"

"No, sir."

Grandpa paused as he took the pitchfork and gunnysack from the truck. "That's good. Well, if the fox is clean, we won't have anything to worry about. If it isn't, well, we'll face that when we get to it."

"What happens if it's not?" Matt asked, handing Duke off to Joshua.

"The dogs will be quarantined," Grandpa said as he lifted the fox with the pitchfork, dropped it into the sack, and threw the bundle into the back of the truck. "We might have to get a couple of shots. That's all."

"Let the dogs loose, and they'll follow us to the house."

The truck bounced along the dirt road through the old peach orchard. Duke loped along behind with ease. Lady, her short legs moving like pistons, managed to keep up.

"Joshua," Grandpa said when they pulled up next to the barn, "you and Matthew lock the dogs in the old hog pen—just in case there's a problem. Put some food and water out there and fresh hay in the shed."

"Matthew, your grandma isn't going to be happy to have Lady and Duke penned up, but it's for their good as well as ours," Grandpa said. "Sometimes we have to do things we don't like—but it's for the best."

Matt felt Grandpa wasn't thinking about the dogs when he said this. He wondered what Grandpa wasn't telling him.

*   *   *

Later, as they waited in the truck outside the veterinarian's office, Grandpa cleared his throat and said, "Matthew, Dr. Johnson took one look at that fox and said without even testing it, he's sure it's rabid. That foam around the mouth pretty much tells the story."

Matt's eyes got big, and he took as deep breath as Grandpa said, "It used to be that if people caught rabies, they'd die a terrible death. But we're lucky. Now all we have to do is take a few shots, and we'll be fine."

Grandpa hesitated and then went on. "You might as well know, Dr. Smith will give you a shot below your belly button.

He paused. Matt wanted to put his fingers in his ears. Every time Grandpa hesitated, it got worse.

"The truth be told, there're five shots. Not all at once, mind you. We'll get the first one today and the other four in the next two weeks," he said as he started the truck.

Matt felt sick. A shot—no, five shots—in his belly! He clutched his stomach as though to protect it from what was to come.

When they pulled up to Dr. Smith's clinic in the small brick building that had once been a church, Grandpa said, "Joshua, you go on in. We'll meet you back here in a little while."

"Where's he going?" Matt asked as Joshua entered the clinic through the doorway with a sign marked *colored* hung above it.

"That's the colored waiting room," Grandpa said. "The white waiting room is around front."

"Why didn't Joshua come with us?" Matt asked when he and Grandpa were seated in the waiting room.

Grandpa looked surprised at the question. "That's just the way it is here," he said. "They have their own churches, their own schools, and their own waiting room at the doctor's office. I don't think I've ever heard anyone object."

"Do you think anybody ever asked?"

Before Grandpa could answer, the door marked *Exam Room* opened and a man in a white coat walked in.

"Mr. Morrison!" Dr. Smith said, extending his right hand to Grandpa. "Let's go ahead and get this procedure started so you and your grandson can get on about your afternoon activities. Come right this way." With a flourish, he ushered Grandpa and Matt into the examining room.

Matt had expected Dr. Smith to be old and gray, and even a little slow, but he was young and obviously full of energy.

"Now I know no one looks forward to a shot," he said as he turned to the counter, holding a tray of bottles, jars with swabs and cotton balls, and small paper bags. "It's always worse thinking about it than it really is. Soooo, let's go ahead and get it over with."

"Mr. Morrison, if you'll take a seat in the waiting room, I'll be with you in just a few minutes."

Grandpa looked surprised. "Don't you want me to, well, you know, hold him or something," he said, reaching out and taking hold of Matt's shoulder.

"Oh no, that won't be necessary, will it?" Dr. Smith asked, turning to Matt.

"No, sir."

"I thought not. See there Mr. Morrison—we'll be just fine," Dr. Smith said as he ushered Grandpa out of the room and closing the door.

With Grandpa gone, Dr. Smith turned to Matt.

"Now then, we haven't been introduced. I'm Dr. Smith, and you are?"

For a moment, Matt was speechless. He had never met anyone quite like Dr. Smith.

"I'm Matt, that is Matthew, Morrison, sir.

"I'm sorry we have to meet under such circumstances, Matt," Dr. Smith said, "but if you'll slip your overalls down and hop up on this exam table, we'll get this over with. Laying down helps your stomach muscles relax," he said, turning back to the counter.

Dr. Smith reached into the sterilizer and took out a syringe and needle. After he loaded the syringe with medication, he swabbed a small area of Matt's stomach below his belly button with alcohol.

"Now, Matt, I want you to take a deep breath, count to ten, and let your breath out slowly. Do that three times."

As Matt was concentrating on letting his breath out the second time, he felt a slight prick as Dr. Smith gave him his first shot.

"There, that wasn't so bad, was it?" Dr. Smith said as he wiped the area with alcohol and applied a Band-Aid.

"No. No, sir, it wasn't," Matt said.

"How about going to the door and asking your grandfather to come in."

After adjusting his overalls, Matt opened the exam room door and said, "Grandpa, Dr. Smith is ready for you."

As Grandpa started through the door, Matt turned to Dr. Smith and asked, "Do you want me to stay and hold him for you?"

Matt could hear Dr. Smith laugh as he closed the door.

*   *   *

Outside in the parking lot, Matt climbed into the back of the pickup truck where Joshua waited with his hat pulled down over his eyes and his back against the cab of the truck.

"Bet you won't play with no more foxes," Joshua remarked.

"Don't think I will," Matt said. "Listen, while we were waiting, I asked Grandpa why there are two waiting rooms. He said, 'That's just being how it is.'"

Joshua was quiet for a few minutes. "When I started school, I asked Mama why there weren't any white chi' ren in my class. She said something about 'separate, but equal.' Daddy says things was separate, but they sure ain't equal. He said maybe someday they would be. Now don't that sound nice?"

Just then, Grandpa stomped out of the doctor's office, climbed in the truck, and slammed the door. He hadn't taken kindly to Matt's offer to hold him while Dr. Smith gave him his shot.

Chapter 13

It didn't take long for word of the adventure with the fox to get around.

When Richard saw Matt later that week, the first thing he said was "What's this I hear tell about you meeting up with a Texas fox?"

"Yeah, we have to get some shots, but Dr. Smith said we'll be okay."

"'We'? Who all has to get shots besides you?"

"Grandpa and Joshua."

"Joshua?"

"Yeah, Joshua. He came along just after I found the fox and went to get Grandpa while I kept Duke and Lady away from it. The dogs are in quarantine, and we're getting shots."

"I think I'd rather be in quarantine," Richard said.

"I would too, but that's not how it works. By the way, I hear there's going to be a festival or something this weekend over in Naples. You going?"

"Sure thing. I guess everybody's going to the Watermelon Festival. Cowboys wear their best western gear and show off their horses. Families dress up in old-timey clothes and ride in hay wagons and buckboards. Just anybody who wants to can join in."

"The Methodist and Baptist ladies always have booths. They'll have the best food you've ever tasted. My mama's been saving her sugar ration stamps so's she can bake her famous pound cake. They'll have enough fried chicken, fried catfish, and barbecue to feed all of

Morris County. And then there'll be potato salad, sweet corn, baked beans, and of course, watermelon. There'll even be churned ice cream to go with all of the pies and cakes. And that's not all. There'll be…"

"That's enough," Matt said with a laugh. "You've made me so hungry I just might have to go home and eat another breakfast."

"There's going to be a carnival over on the used car lot too. Don said he saw a tattooed lady with a bi-i-i-g snake around her neck at a carnival over in Mt. Pleasant last year. Wonder if they'll have a strong man or a tattooed lady."

"Wow, that would be something. Maybe they'll have a sword-swallower. What do you think?"

"Could be. Oh, I almost forgot the best thing—the egg toss!"

"What's an egg toss?" asked Matt.

"If you don't know, you'll just have to wait until Saturday to find out. Well, I'd better get back and finish my chores. See ya later."

"Sure thing," Matt said.

*　　*　　*

"I need your help," Grandma said to him the next morning. "There's some things down in the root cellar I'm taking to the Watermelon Festival tomorrow to sell at the Methodist Church missionary circle's booth. All the money we make will go for our mission work in the Congo. Now bring along one of those baskets."

Grandma led him outside to what looked like a mound of dirt with a door in it.

"Help me open this door. It's heavy."

"I'll say it's heavy," Matt said, giving the door a tug. "What's in here anyway?" he asked as he peered through the opening and down the steps that led to a small, low ceiling room.

"Grandpa dug it so we'd have someplace to go when a tornado hits. He built the shelves on the walls for the preserves I put up. It's dark and cool and keeps things right good."

Grandma loaded their baskets with cucumber pickles, tomato relish, and plum preserves as she spoke.

"What's going to be at the festival besides food?" Matt asked.

"Well, I believe one of the Baptist ladies' circles has been making aprons to sell. Then there's a man who does some pretty fine leatherwork. He usually has belts and billfolds. Then there'll be the missionary circle booths. And I imagine there'll be pony rides for the little ones."

"Richard Wright said there's going to be a carnival too."

"I believe I heard something about that. There hasn't been one in Omaha since before the war. Those carnival people aren't from around here. Some of them might not be as honest as they should be. If you go over there, be careful."

"Yes, 'um," he said.

The next morning, Matt put on the new blue-checkered shirt he had bought with some of the money he had earned. The cuffs of his freshly laundered overalls had narrowed. At the rate he was growing, he'd need new ones before summer was over.

He helped load the car and sat in the back seat steadying the baskets of preserves. Grandma had carefully wrapped the jars in newspaper to keep them from breaking as they drove over the washboard-rutted road. Grandpa wanted to put the baskets in the trunk, but Grandma wouldn't hear of it.

When they got to Naples, Matt looked around while he helped Grandpa unload the car near the food booths. Under nearby trees, men were setting up tables and chairs. Grandma said there was unofficial competition between the Methodist and Baptist ladies to see who had the best-decorated booths. But everybody knew it wasn't the brightly colored crepe paper decorations that attracted the crowds. It was the platters and bowls filled with the offerings of the best cooks in Morris County.

Matt fingered the dollar he had stuck deep in his pocket. His mother usually gave him 35¢ a week for an allowance. With that, he could go to the Saturday movie matinée, buy a bag of popcorn, and have enough left for a comic book. Having a dollar gave him so many options, he couldn't decide what to buy.

As he walked over to the barbecue pit where some of the boys he had worked with were standing, Matt looked around for the Wilson brothers. He wondered if Jake would be wearing the red bandana.

"Hey, you're just in time. Pretty soon there'll be a long line," Don said when Matt got to the barbecue pit.

"Don't it smell great? They've been cookin' all night," Jim said. "As soon as the parade's over, the booth'll open.

"Matt, you ever had Texas barbecue? It's the best there is," Richard said.

"No, I haven't, but I think I'll wait a while. I'm going over to the carnival. Come over when you've finished eating."

"You can't go now! The parade's gettin' ready to start! My cousin Tom's ridin' his palomino stallion—looks just like Roy Roger's Trigger! Listen, you can hear the band now!" Richard said.

Around the corner leading the parade came the uniformed color guard with the American and the Texas State flags held high. The Naples High School band, following close behind, struck up a lively march.

Bringing up the rear was a group of mounted women and men led by Richard's cousin Tom on his palomino. Some of the women were wearing leather riding skirts; others wore jeans. As they rode by, all the riders doffed their Stetsons to the cheering crowd.

"They'll all be riding in the rodeo—bucking horses and bulls!" Richard exclaimed. "I wanted to give it a try, but my dad said I'm too young. You just wait. In a few years, I'll be riding right along with them."

"You mean those women are going to ride bucking horses and bulls?" asked Matt.

"Well, no. They'll be riding in the barrel race. Seeing how fast they can ride a figure eight around two barrels without knocking the barrels over. Them cow ponies can almost turn on a dime."

The parade continued down the street followed by the "clean-up" crew with a wheelbarrow, brooms, and shovels. A rodeo clown and his assistants quickly removed any "souvenirs" the horses may have left.

"Before you go over to the carnival, you've just got to watch the egg toss," Richard said. "Jack was last year's champion. I hear tell Don's been practicing, but practice don't always make perfect with the egg toss."

Matt followed Richard down the block to where a crowd had gathered. They were watching two boys and a man who were standing in the middle of the street where lines had been drawn. One of the boys reached in a basket the man was holding and took out an egg. He tossed the egg to the other boy. Then they both stepped back to the next line, widening the distance between them. The second boy threw the egg back.

"That doesn't look so hard," Matt said.

"Just you wait!" Richard responded, watching the boys intently.

With each exchange, the gap widened between the boys and the egg was tossed higher. The crowd murmured as one of the boys caught the egg with a backward sweeping motion.

"That's Bob. He's good!" said Richard. "I'll bet he's been practicing."

Just then, Bob tossed the egg high and long. His opponent reached backward above his head and caught the egg—only to have it disintegrate in his hand. Yellow "goo" ran down his arm. The crowd laughed and applauded as the referee offered the loser a towel.

"Wow!" Matt exclaimed. "The egg was raw! I thought it was boiled!"

"It's even more fun if people think there's a rotten egg in the basket," Richard said. "Sometime there is, and sometime there isn't. Now, let's get back over to the barbecue pit. I'm about to starve."

"You go ahead. I'm going over at the carnival first," Matt said.

"Don't be long or there might not be any left!" Richard said. "We're a hungry bunch!"

Chapter 14

Matt headed down the street to the vacant lot where the carnival had set up. The booths and tents were worn and faded. Paint was hard to get, and canvas for tents was not available because of the war. He noticed all the people running the concessions were women or older men. Most young men were away at war.

Music was coming from a merry-go-round at the end of a row of booths. Matt walked slowly past the booths where all sorts of prizes were offered. When he saw a man standing in front of the sharp-shooter booth with a rifle at his shoulder, Matt stopped to watch. A bell rang, and a mechanical duck fell over every time the man pulled the trigger.

"Here you go, young feller," the man said, offering Matt the rifle. "You can do the same thing and win a teddy bear for your girlfriend."

He pointed to a shelf at the back of the booth filled with stuffed animals, coffee mugs with TEXAS printed on them, ladies painted fans, and bright bandanas.

"It'll only cost you fifteen cents for five shots."

"I don't have a girlfriend, but I'd like to try for that painted fan for my grandma. The only thing is, I've never shot a rifle before."

"There's nothing to it. Tell you what, I'll let you take two shots for free, just to show you how easy it is."

"Okay, I'll give it a try."

Matt pushed his hat back on his head, picked up the rifle and put it to his shoulder. He looked down the sight and carefully squeezed the trigger. To his surprise, the bell rang, and a duck fell over. The same thing happened the second time.

"Did you see this young feller?" the man asked the people who had gathered to watch. "He's a natural born sharp-shooter."

"Here's my fifteen cents." Matt handed the man the money and started to put the rifle to his shoulder again.

"That gun's all out of bullets. Take this one." The man picked up another rifle and handed it to Matt.

Taking careful aim, Matt pulled the trigger. The bell rang and a duck fell over. He was feeling pretty confident. But that good feeling disappeared when the last four shots missed their mark.

"Well, I guess that's that," Matt said.

"Don't give up so easy, young feller. You're a natural, you just had a few unlucky shots. Give it another try," the man said.

"No, I don't think so," Matt replied.

As Matt turned to walk away from the booth, he heard someone in the crowd say, "Did you hear the man say he was a natural? A natural what?"

"Yeah, some sharp-shooter. He couldn't shoot his way out of a paper bag."

It was Jake Wilson. He was looking at his brother Ray, but he was talking loud enough for the rest of the people who had gathered to hear his insults.

Ray laughed, and some of the bystanders joined in.

Matt wished the ground would open up and swallow him. As he walked away from the booth, he could feel the heat from his face and ears.

Jake and Ray followed behind him laughing.

Matt turned and stood his ground. He didn't hear what Jake said next because he was concentrating so hard on the bandana Jake was wearing.

"Where'd you get that bandana?" Matt demanded.

"Found it, if it's any of your business."

"Where'd you find it? I lost one just like it."

"Yeah, well, that's just too bad. Don't forget—finders' keepers, losers weepers."

"It looks like you're the weeper," Ray said with a sneer.

"Besides, you can't prove it's yours," Jake said. "Be a good boy and go take a ride on the merry-go-round."

As they talked, Jake and Ray boxed Matt in between them. He tried to step back from Jake, but Ray tripped him. Matt fell sprawling on the ground.

"Hey, what's going on here?"

It was the man from the shack. He looked really mad.

"I've been looking all over for you two. We have…ah…work to be doing, and here I find you horsing around. You two get in the truck."

"Sure, Mr. Crawford," Jake said, stepping away from Matt.

"These boys don't mean no harm. Just joshing 'round," Mr. Crawford said as he extended a hand to Matt and helped him up.

"You two still standing there? Didn't I tell you to get in the truck?" he said, looking over his shoulder at Jake and Ray. The smile he had displayed for Matt's benefit became a menacing frown.

"I'll be seeing you again," Jake said to Matt as he turned to walk away.

"That's fine with me," Matt replied.

"Hey, what was that all about?" Tob asked as he and the other boys came running up.

"If you need some help with those two, just say so," Don said.

He was the lightweight in the group but known for not backing down from anyone.

"Thanks. Don't worry about it. I'll take care of it," Matt said, even though he hadn't the least idea how. "How was the barbecue?"

"I'm going back for more… Pork's best… No, chicken is…you can't beat the beef ribs" came a chorus of replies from the boys.

"I think I'll go find out for myself. See you fellows later."

As he walked toward the festival grounds, the hot, still air wrapped around him like an unwanted blanket. He mopped his forehead with his bandana and settled his hat on his head.

"What was you doin' tusslin' with the big boys?"

Matt looked around to see who had spoken. There was Joshua, leaning against a pecan tree by the side of the road.

"They had some smart things to say about my shooting. Then I asked Jake where he got his bandana. I'd have taken care of them if that man hadn't come along."

"Sure you would have. You might have growed some this summer, but you ain't big enough to take on those two by yourself."

"Do you know that man with the truck? Jake called him Mr. Crawford. He's the same one who was at the creekers' shack."

"I seen him down at the fillin' station but don't know who he is. His truck has an Arkansas tag on it," Joshua said.

"Maybe he's a relative of the Wilsons. That would explain why Jake and Ray are hanging around with him. But if he's family, why do they call him 'Mr. Crawford'? I don't think I'd want him in my family. He looks like he could be real mean."

"Well, we don't gets to pick our family…just our friends. Course, friends come and go, but you always got your family, so I guess it's good to be friends with your family too."

"Joshua, I'm not quite sure what you said, but I think you're right," Matt said with a laugh.

"How about going fishing tomorrow morning before it gets too hot? You want to meet me down by the creek?"

"We'd better go early. If it's as hot as it is today, the fish'll be as deep as they can get trying to stay cool. Bet we gets a storm this afternoon," Joshua said. He shaded his eyes with his hand and looked to the northwest. A thin dark line lay on the horizon. "That don't look good," he said. "Guess I'll be heading to the house. See you in the mornin'."

"Sure thing," Matt said.

Matt followed his nose to the barbecue booth. The tantalizing aroma hung heavy in the hot, still air. In a few minutes, his plate was piled high with all three kinds of barbecue, baked beans, sweet corn, and light bread. After paying his $.45, he picked up a big cup of sweet iced tea and found a seat.

When he finished eating, he took his empty plate to the overflowing garbage can.

"Son, how about helping empty those cans," one of the men called from the barbecue booth.

"Yes, sir," Matt replied. He looked around for other helpers and, seeing no one, set to work by himself. The cans stank. By the time he had them emptied in the back of the garbage truck, he was glad there were only four cans.

He cleaned up the ground around the tables and where the cans were placed.

"That was a good job. Thanks for the help," the man said as he handed Matt a tall cup of sweet iced tea.

"You're welcome," Matt said. He headed for the shade of the trees behind the booths and sat with his back against one of the oaks while he drank the tea.

As the afternoon wore on, the cloud line on the horizon built and darkened. The sky seemed artificially bright and sunny ahead of the weather front. An occasional low rumble of thunder could be heard in the distance.

"Matthew, the weather's gettin' ready to turn bad. We're going to close down the fair so everybody can get home. I want you and Grandma to ride home with Mrs. Wright and Richard. Mr. Wright and I are going to stay and help take down the booths."

"Don't you want us to stay and help?" Matt asked.

"No, I'd rather you go home to help your grandma. By the way, Mr. Brown told me what a good job you did cleaning up around the barbecue stand."

Grandpa didn't say any more, but Matt could tell he was pleased by the report from Mr. Brown.

Matt loaded Grandma's empty baskets in the trunk of the car before climbing in the back seat with Richard. As they drove past the carnival, he looked for Jake and Ray and the man with the blue truck. He didn't see them or the pickup. What kind of work did the man want them to do?

Chapter 15

The ride home was hot, even though all the windows in the car were rolled down. There was no cooling breeze. Inky-black clouds filled the horizon and pushed against the bright blue sky. There was a sense of urgency and expectation in the oppressive air.

"Thank you for the ride home, Thelma," Grandma said as they pulled into the drive.

"Matthew, hurry in the house and close the windows while I get the chickens in the hen house. When you finish, come help me take the clothes off the line. I don't think we have much time to spare," Grandma said as the Wrights drove away.

After Matt closed the last window, he headed out the back door to the clothesline to help Grandma. The wind had begun to blow, making it hard for her to catch hold of the clothes. The clothespin bag was bobbing on the line. Only the weight of the pins kept it from flying off.

Matt had grabbed a pair of Grandpa's overalls just as a bolt of lightning struck down by the creek. The thunder was deafening. The wind blew so hard, Matt could hardly stand.

"Get in the root cellar," Grandma yelled as a hard driving rain pelted them. She clutched the clothes in her arms and began to run. She hadn't gone many steps when she tripped on a sheet trailing on the ground. Matt helped her to her feet, but he couldn't save the clothes that were caught by the wind and dashed to earth by the rain.

The wind at their backs pushed them along. When they reached the cellar door, they fell to their knees. Matt took hold of the iron ring and pulled. The door didn't budge. Another tug opened the door just a crack. On the third try, the door yielded enough for Matt to get his shoulder inside and push it open. He and Grandma scrambled down the stairs as the door slammed shut behind them.

After the roar of the wind, the cellar seemed unnaturally quiet. Then Matt heard the sound of rocks pounding against the door.

"Grandma, what's that sound?"

"It must be hailstones. It's a blessing we weren't caught out in the open. Last year we had a hailstorm that dented cars, broke windshields, and tore up house roofs. It can do a lot of damage to whatever's in the fields too—crops or animals. I hope Bonnie and the mules hid under the trees."

"What about Lady and Duke?"

"They were both going under the house when I came out of the chicken yard. Animals seem to know when to take cover. I just hope your grandpa's all right."

Matt sat on the stairs and listened to the sound of hail beating on the door and the muffled boom of thunder. After what seemed like a very long time, all was quiet.

Hail rolled off the root cellar door when Matt pushed it open. The air outside felt cold and damp. Pellets of ice lay on the ground. Some were as large as baseballs. Matt could hear the low rumble of distant thunder from the departing storm.

By the time they gathered all the clothes they could find, it was almost dark. One of the sheets hung from the upper limb of an oak.

"I'm sure your grandpa will figure out a way to get that sheet down. I'll wash everything in the morning and see what's missing. Let's just put the clothes to soak in the washtub in the barn," Grandma said.

"Matthew, open the back barn doors and see if Bonnie and the mules have come up. You can put some food in the troughs for them. There's no telling when your grandpa will be home."

Matt removed the bar from across the barn doors and pushed them open. Bonnie was waiting patiently to be let in. Millie and Jack were standing off a short distance. Through the gathering gloom, Matt could see John Henry and Dusty making their way up the well-worn path from the outer pasture.

"Grandma, I don't see Joe and Jenny."

"I imagine they'll be up before long. Let's finish the chores so we can go in and have some supper."

Because the power lines were down, they ate a cold supper by the light of a kerosene lamp.

It was late when Grandpa finally came home. Tired and bedraggled, he paused a moment on the back porch to take off his mud-caked boots. His clothes were wet and stained with mud.

"I've never seen such a mess," Grandpa said as he lowered himself into a kitchen chair.

"We got the booths taken down and were just putting away the last of the chairs and tables in the church basement when the wind and rain hit. Just about that time somebody said, 'Sounds like the Cotton Belt is running a mite early.'"

"Well, it wasn't the train—it was a twister. We found out it took the roof off the peach shed by the train track in Omaha, skipped across the road, and hit the schoolhouse on the hill. It took out three walls of that school as pretty as you please. I'll bet there're bricks from that building fallin' all over Morris County."

"How awful," Grandma said. "Was anybody hurt?"

"Not that I know of. We checked the shed and what was left of the school but didn't find anybody. When it's daylight, they'll be able to see what other damage was done. Any problems here?"

"Other than having to do the washing over, I don't know of anything. There's a sheet in a tree that we couldn't reach. We had a lot of hail, and there is no telling what that might have done. Of course, it was almost dark when we came out of the root cellar, so we couldn't see much," Grandma replied.

"Grandpa, I saw only four of the mules when I fed them. Grandma thought the other two were just slow coming up."

"If they haven't showed up by morning, we'll go lookin' for them," Grandpa said.

Before he went to bed, Matt took carrots out to the mules. John Henry, Millie, Jack, and Dusty crowded against the fence; but there was still no sign of Jenny or Joe.

Grandpa was standing by the corral when Matt came out the next morning. The sun was still below the horizon, but there was enough light to see there were only four mules in the corral.

"I was hoping they'd be here," Grandpa said. "Don't let these mules out until we know what's happened to the others. Get in the truck, and we'll drive down to the lower pasture and have a look. They could have been hit by lightnin' or a tree might have blowed over on 'em. Almost anything can happen when you have a storm like that."

They drove along the path the mules usually took to the lower pasture. There were a few limbs down from the trees that lined the fence, but there was no sign of the mules. Then Matt spotted something.

"Look, Grandpa, there's a hole in the fence."

Grandpa stopped. He and Matt got out of the truck to get a better look. Six strands of barbed wire lay curled up on the ground at the foot of a fence post.

Grandpa picked up one of the pieces of wire and looked at the end.

"Somebody cut my fence!" There was surprise and anger in Grandpa's voice.

"That's how the mules got out." Grandpa paused. "No, dang-nab-it, they didn't get out. They were helped out."

Grandpa headed for the truck. Matt was right behind him. Grandpa started the truck, and they were headed back to the house before Matt could close the door.

When they got to the house, Grandpa stormed through the kitchen and headed for the telephone in the living room.

"Did you find the mules?" Grandma asked.

Before Matt could answer, Grandpa was back in the kitchen.

"The phone's dead. The lines must still be down. I'm goin' to town to find the sheriff," Grandpa said. On his way out the door, he told Grandma what they'd found.

"I'll go with you, Grandpa," Matt said.

"No, you stay here with your grandma. With all the storm damage, there's no telling where I'll find the sheriff."

"Be careful. Don't do anything foolish," Grandma called after Grandpa.

"I do hope the sheriff finds those rustlers before your grandpa does," she said to Matt "There's no telling what he'll do when he's riled up."

Matt knew only too well how Grandpa could act when he was "riled up." He almost felt sorry for any rustlers Grandpa caught.

While he was doing his chores, Matt kept watching the road in hopes that Grandpa would come back and make him part of a posse. Did they still have posses in Texas like they had in the Saturday westerns? If they did, would they drive cars or ride horses?

He was still thinking about this when Joshua showed up with two fishing poles on his shoulder.

"Grandma, I've finished my chores. Is it okay if I go fishing with Joshua?" Matt called from the back porch.

"I don't see why not," Grandma said. "I'll ring the porch bell if I need you for anything."

The boys walked single file through the woods toward the creek.

"That was some storm we had yesterday," Joshua said, looking back over his shoulder at Matt. "We had some big hail over our way. It knocked down some of the corn. Mama said she was glad it wasn't any worse."

"Grandma and I went down in the root cellar. You should have seen what happened to the washing. Clothes were blown everywhere. Did you see that sheet up in the tree? It's too high for us to reach. There are still a few pieces of wash missing. That was bad enough, but the worst thing is two of the mules didn't come up last night. Grandpa and I went looking for them at first light this morning. We found where somebody had cut the fence in the lower pasture. Grandpa sure is mad. He's gone to town to find the sheriff because the phone lines are still down and he couldn't call him."

"Hey, look, the creek's way up the banks. Looks like all that rain really filled it up," Matt said.

"That's not good for fishing. It muddies the water. It'll be better in a day or two when it's not running so high," said Joshua.

"Let's give it a try anyway. We might be lucky."

The boys had just dropped their lines in the water and settled down on the bank when a faint but familiar sound came from upstream. *E-E-E-E-E-E hu-hu-hu-hu-hu.*

Chapter 16

The boys looked at each other.

"The mules!" they yelled in unison.

Matt and Joshua scrambled to their feet and began to run along the creek bank toward the direction of the sound. They hadn't gone far before Matt pulled up short.

"We're making too much noise. Whoever has the mules might have posted a lookout."

"How do you know it's your grandpa's mules? Might be somebody else's."

"Don't you see? Whoever stole the mules is keeping them in the corral at the creeker's shack. It's got to be Mr. Crawford, the man I saw at the shack. He was asking about the mules when we were delivering the melons in town. And when he got mad at Jake and Ray at the carnival…I'll bet the work he was talking about was stealing Grandpa's mules."

"You just might be right. But what you gonna do?" Joshua asked.

"We're going down there and see what's going on. Then we can figure out how to get them back."

"What do you mean 'we'? You crazy? You told me the last time you were there the man had a rifle. We don't have no rifle—not even a slingshot. You've seen too many westerns. I don't plan to be in no shoot-out."

"We're not going to be in a shoot-out. We're just gonna take a look. We'll let Grandpa and the sheriff figure out what to do next," Matt said.

"That's different. I don't mind looking. Just as long as we don't look too close."

Joshua reluctantly followed Matt to the log footbridge that lay across the creek.

Matt tested the log to make sure the rising water hadn't washed out the bank. When it held, he carefully worked his way across. Joshua hesitated then followed.

They stopped at the path to the shack and listened. Voices could be heard, but they were too far away to hear what was being said. They crept through the undergrowth until they could see the shack in the clearing. The blue pickup truck and a truck with an enclosed livestock trailer were parked by the shack.

Mr. Crawford and another man stood on the porch arguing. The Wilson boys were sitting on the steps listening to the discussion. In the corral were Jenny and Joe and three head of cattle.

"I tell you, we should wait until after dark. It's safer that way," Mr. Crawford said.

"You heard the racket that mule was making. If he keeps that up, somebody is sure to hear him. The sooner we get on the road, the better," the other man said.

"Joe didn't get his carrot this morning, and he's letting the world know about it," Matt whispered to Joshua.

The boys retreated to the creek bank.

"Let's go to your grandpa's and wait for him," said Joshua. "Maybe he'll bring the sheriff back with him."

"No, we can't wait. You heard what they said. One of them wants to load the mules and cattle up right now and leave. By the time we can find Grandpa and he gets the sheriff, they could be on their way to Arkansas or Louisiana," said Matt. "We can't take a chance on them waiting 'til dark. I have an idea. You stay here and keep an eye on things while I go to the house. I'll ride Millie back so it won't take long."

"You're gonna leave me here? What good's that gonna do? You don't expect me to go stand in the middle of the road if they try to leave, do you?" Joshua asked. "'Cause if you do, you've got another think coming."

"No, I don't. But if they leave before I get back, you can tell me how long they've been gone. Then when we find Grandpa and the sheriff, we can tell them how long they've been on the road."

"I don't know what good that'll do," Joshua said. He hesitated a moment. "All right. I'll watch, but watch is all I'm goin' t' do."

"Okay, that's fine," Matt said as he turned to make his way over the creek.

Running as fast as he could, Matt took the shortcut through the old peach orchard. He was just about out of breath by the time he reached the house.

"Grandma, we've found the mules at the creekers' shack," Matt yelled as he ran in the back door. "Have you seen Grandpa? Did he find the sheriff?" There was no answer.

He ran to his bedroom and pulled the rawhide-covered keg from the back of the closet. Tucking it under his arm, he headed out the back door to the barn where he found Grandma sorting through the salvaged laundry.

"Grandma, is the power back on? You've got to call the sheriff and tell him we've found the mules and some cattle at the creekers' shack. Some men are getting ready to load them up. I've got to stop them," Matt said as he grabbed one of the mules' bridles off a hook.

"The power is on, and I'll call the sheriff, but it's too dangerous for you to try and stop those men. Stay here until your grandpa gets home or the sheriff comes," Grandma said.

"I can't. Joshua is watching, and he expects me back. If we don't do something, Grandpa might never see his mules again."

He walked quietly into the corral and offered the mules some of the carrots he had picked up on his way through the kitchen. When each mule had a carrot, Matt scratched Millie's ear and spoke softly as he put the bridle on her. He had ridden Millie enough that he had gotten the hang of mounting bareback without help. After he was up, he rode over to the fence and picked up the keg he had left on a post.

Grandma opened the gate for him.

"I'll send Millie back home as soon as I get to the creek," Matt called over his shoulder as he leaned forward, flipped the reins against Millie's neck, and gave her a nudge with his heels.

She seemed to sense the urgency and moved out at a smart pace. It wasn't an easy ride, but Millie got him back to the creek much quicker than he could have made it on foot. And right now, he had to make every minute count.

As soon as he got to the creek, Matt slid to the ground, put the reins around Millie's neck, turned her toward home, and gave her a slap on the rump. He was pretty sure she would go home.

When he started across the log, the keg under his arm pulled him off-balanced. He could feel himself leaning dangerously to one side. This was no time to fall in the creek. A splash might alert the rustlers. He pulled the keg in toward his chest and stuck out his other arm as a counterbalance. When he had steadied himself, he made his way carefully to the other side.

"Anything happen while I was gone?" Matt asked as he knelt down beside Joshua in the underbrush. He could see Jake and Ray standing by the corral, but the two men weren't in sight.

"I think the second man won the argument. The last I could hear, they was planning to eat something then load up and leave. I'm glad you're back. Just what is this great plan of yours?"

"It should really be easy," Matt said. He showed Joshua the keg and explained how it worked and how the mules had broken down the corral and gotten out when his daddy used it.

"The way I figure it, if we make this thing roar a couple of times, the mules and cattle will panic, break down the corral, and escape. The rustlers won't even know we're here. They'll think a catamount is down by the creek."

"What if they decide to come down here and shoot that catamount?" Joshua asked.

"Don't worry, they'll be too busy trying to catch the mules and the cattle. We can have this thing roar a couple of more times just to make sure they won't catch them. We'll be over the creek and on our way home in no time."

"Hey, sounds like somebody's coming," Joshua said.

The sound of a motor came from the direction of the dirt road that led to the shack. A familiar truck came in sight.

"Oh no. It's Grandpa," Matt groaned.

The truck had hardly stopped rolling when Grandpa was out the door. He was moving so fast, he was practically running.

"What do you boys think you're doing with my mules?" he yelled at Jake and Ray as he headed for the corral.

"Grandma sure was right," said Matt, shaking his head.

"How's that?" Joshua asked.

"She said, 'People can do some really dumb things when they're mad.'"

The words were hardly out of Matt's mouth when the two men appeared on the porch of the cabin. Mr. Crawford held a sandwich, but the other man held a rifle, and it was pointed at Grandpa.

"Hold it right there," the gunman yelled.

Grandpa turned and started back toward his truck.

"I said, 'Hold it right there,'" the man yelled again as he ran down the steps.

Grandpa stopped and turned around slowly. He didn't say anything, but Matt could tell by the droop of Grandpa's shoulders and the way he stood that he didn't see where he had any choice but to do as the man ordered.

"Tell you what," Grandpa said. "You drive out of here and leave my mules and the cattle, and we'll forget about this."

"I don't think so," Mr. Crawford said. "We've gone to too much trouble to give them up that easy. What do you think we ought to do with him, Hank?" he asked the man with the rifle.

"If he's out looking, there must others looking too. Can't leave him here," Hank replied. "We can take him with us and drop him off on a stretch of highway between here and the state line. By the time somebody finds him, we'll be long gone."

"You boys get some rope and tie him to that tree," Mr. Crawford said to Jake and Ray. "He'll be out of the way, but we can keep an eye on him."

They tied Grandpa to a sapling that was growing by the porch.

Matt and Joshua felt like they were watching one of the Saturday movies they were always talking about. The good guy had come rushing in to capture the rustlers and save the day, but something had gone terribly wrong. Instead of doing the rescuing, the hero needed to be rescued.

"Do you think they're gonna shoot him?" Joshua asked.

"I don't know, but we can't wait to find out. We've got to do something now," Matt replied.

He picked up the keg and gently pulled his fingers down the cord. A low resonant sound came from the keg. The mules threw up their heads and looked around. The cattle moved restlessly.

"What was that?" asked Jake, who had just finished tying Grandpa to the tree.

"I don't know, but it sure made those critters restless. Let's get them loaded before anything else happens," Mr. Crawford replied. "I'll back the truck to the gate, and we'll load them up."

Matt watched until Mr. Crawford was in the truck. Then he motioned for Joshua to follow him. They moved quietly through the undergrowth toward the back of the shack.

"Take the keg and make it roar like I showed you. Keep moving, so they can't locate you. I'll go around back, come up alongside of the shack, and cut Grandpa loose," Matt said as he reached for his pocketknife.

"Matt," Joshua said.

"Yeah?"

"You said we were just gonna take a look and see what was going on. I think we're way past lookin' and seein'."

"I know, but we can't just turn around and go home. I sure didn't plan on Grandpa showin' up."

Matt took cover behind a tree. Even though he was expecting the roar from the keg, when it came, it sent a shiver down his spine and made the hair on the back of his neck stand up.

The mules threw up their heads, their eyes rolling, as they raced frantically around the corral. The cattle bellowed and pushed against the enclosure.

Jake and Ray looked around in confusion.

"Get that truck up to the gate. You boys calm those animals down. We've got to get out of here," Hank yelled. He picked up a coil of rope from the porch and ran toward the corral.

The running and yelling only served to further panic the livestock.

While the rustlers were concentrating on the corral, Matt made a dash across the clearing to the back of the shack. He moved along the side of the building to a spot just behind the tree where Grandpa was tied.

One more roar from the keg and pandemonium broke loose. The cattle frantically tried to climb the corral fence. The mules lunged against the enclosure. With the sound of splintering wood, the corral sides gave way.

Livestock scattered in all directions.

Matt ran up behind Grandpa and cut the rope.

"Where did you come from?" Grandpa asked as he looked over his shoulder to see who had freed him.

"Never mind. We've got to get out of here," Matt replied.

Chapter 17

Mr. Crawford and Hank looked over from the corral.

"Hey! Stop right there. You ain't going nowhere," Hank yelled.

He ran toward the porch where he had left his rifle leaning against a post, but Matt got there first and grabbed the rifle.

"If you come any closer, I'll shoot," Matt yelled as he whirled around to face Hank.

"Now, boy, you know you won't do no such thing. Just give me the rifle and nobody'll get hurt," Hank said in a friendly tone. Moving slowly up the steps, he held out his hand.

The others stopped where they were, but when Hank started talking, they began to move closer.

"Y'all better do like Matt says," Joshua said, coming around the corner of the shack. "He's a crack shot."

Hank hesitated and then backed down the steps.

Joshua jumped up on the porch and walked up behind Matt.

"Do ya wants to give me the rifle so's you can finish cutting Mr. Morrison free?" Joshua asked in a casual tone.

Without taking his eyes off Hank, Matt stepped aside and handed Joshua the rifle. He was only too glad to give it up. After all, the only gun Matt had shot was at the carnival. Joshua had told Matt he had been hunting squirrel since he was "knee-high to a June bug." That qualified him to hold a rifle on the rustlers as far as Matt was concerned.

Matt finished cutting Grandpa loose just as three cars appeared on the dirt road. The sheriff, Texas Rangers, and some other men stepped out of the cars with guns drawn.

"Put that rifle down and step away with your hands up," the sheriff called.

Joshua laid the rifle on the porch and went to stand with Matt.

"It's okay, Sheriff, he's one of us," Grandpa yelled.

"Mr. Morrison, is that you? What's going on here?" the sheriff asked as he holstered his gun and walked over to where Grandpa, Matt, and Joshua were standing.

"Well, sir, these two boys just saved my hide and captured the rustlers," Grandpa said. "They'll have to tell you what's been going on because I'm not sure. I came in at the tail end of it all."

Matt told the sheriff and the Rangers how he and Joshua had been fishing and heard the mules.

"Joe hadn't had his morning carrot, and he was putting up a fuss," Matt said with a laugh. "If he hadn't made so much noise, we'd never have found him and the rest. They'd most likely be on their way to Arkansas."

"Well, if you boys hadn't been here, I'd most likely be on my way to Arkansas too," said Grandpa. "They said they were going to drop me alongside the highway, but I don't know whether that was going to be dead or alive. I'm sure glad I didn't have to find out."

"Mr. Morrison, I'll want you and the boys to come down to my office and make an official statement about what all went on here," the sheriff said.

The Rangers handcuffed the rustlers and put them in the cars.

Matt walked over to the car where Jake and Ray sat slumped in the back seat.

"I think you have something that belongs to me," he said as he reached inside the car and took the red bandana from around Jake's neck. "Who's the weeper now?"

Jake had lost all his bluster. He didn't say anything but turned his face away from Matt.

The sheriff looked over at the cars where the rustlers waited. "I guess those boys hadn't counted on what would happen when they got caught," he said. "Their mama won't be able to get them off this time. There's no doubting the evidence. Ray'll end up in reform school. Jake's old enough to go to prison. Of course, he might get lucky. The judge could give him a choice between joining the army or going to prison. If he's smart, he'll take the army."

"Sheriff, the mules they had are mine," Grandpa said. "I'm hoping they'll find their way home. From the brands, I'd say the cattle came from the Paulson ranch. Mr. Paulson'll likely want to send over a couple of hands to round them up," Grandpa said. "If they follow my mules in, I'll let him know."

"That'll be fine. I'll see y'all tomorrow at my office for your statements. Say about ten o'clock?"

Grandpa turned to Matt. "That'll give us time to do some chores and look for those mules if they haven't shown up."

Matt had been hoping that after all of the excitement of the last few days, he could sleep late in the morning, but no such luck. There was always something that needed to be done on the farm.

"Boys, get in the truck, and we'll get on back to the house. We need to let Grandma know what's happened. She'll be worried."

Matt and Joshua climbed in the bed of the pickup and sat with their backs against the cab. Exhaustion set in as the tension and excitement drained away.

Joshua was sitting with his knees pulled up, his arms folded across his knees and his forehead resting on his arms. His muffled voice reached Matt. "Remind me to teach you something about guns sometime."

"What do you mean?" Matt asked.

He raised his head and looked at Matt. "The rifle safety was on. You couldn't have shot anybody if you'd had to. Good thing Hank didn't notice."

Matt felt nauseous. If Hank had noticed, all three of them might have been on their way to Arkansas instead of on their way home to supper.

When they stopped at Joshua's house to drop him off, his mother was standing on the porch. Grandpa told her what happened.

"I've been worried about where that boy had got off to. I knowed he'd been gone too long to just be fishin'. Lawd 'a'mercy, you just never know what them chil'ren are gonna get into. Thank you for bringing him home, Mr. Morrison. I'll see to it he's ready in the morning to go with you to talk to the sheriff," Mrs. Williams said.

Grandpa and Matt rode home in silence.

They pulled up into the drive, and Grandpa killed the engine. He sat looking straight ahead with both hands on the steering wheel. Finally, he looked at Matt and said, "I've never spent such a summer in all my life. I don't know whether you've made me feel younger or taken ten years off my life. I guess only time will tell. Come on, son, let's go tell your grandma what we've been up to."

"Yes, sir," Matt said. The grin on his face was almost as wide as Grandpa's.

Chapter 18

Joshua was at the kitchen door just before ten o'clock the next morning.

"You didn't have to come over. Grandpa said we'd pick you up on the way to town," Matt said as he opened the screened door.

"I know, but I had to get out of that house. Mama kept talkin' about how bad things happen when you runs with the wrong crowd. I told her, 'Mama, I ain't running with no rustlers.'"

"What'd she say about that?"

"Something about how all mamas worry about their chi'ren no matter how big they get. She should know she don't need to worry. Why, I don't even help myself to stray watermelons," Joshua said.

"Well, you might not have helped yourself to stray watermelons, but it sure didn't seem to bother your conscience to eat one. Did I tell you Grandma served watermelon that night for dessert? I couldn't tell her I'd already eaten half a watermelon. I thought I'd die."

Both boys were laughing when Grandpa came into the kitchen.

"Let's get on over to Daingerfield so we can tell the sheriff what happened yesterday," Grandpa said, taking his hat off the rack as he started toward the back door. Matt picked up his hat on the way out.

Once on the porch, as though on signal, all three put their hats on and headed for the truck. Matt thought they looked like real cowboys. Well, not quite. They weren't wearing six-guns, and they weren't riding horses. But that was okay—they'd caught the bad guys.

When they pulled up to the curb, a rusty pickup was the only vehicle parked in front of the sheriff's office.

"That old rattletrap looks like it would hardly make it to the corner," Matt said.

A man dressed in faded blue overalls and wearing a worn Stetson got out of the truck and went into the office ahead of them.

Matt and Joshua followed Grandpa inside. The man they'd seen in the rusty pickup was talking with a woman whose gray hair was pulled up in a bun on top of her head. As she smiled and nodded, she tucked a stray wisp of hair behind her ear.

Grandpa walked over and spoke to the woman and the man. Matt was too busy looking at the wanted posters on the bulletin board to hear what they were talking about.

"Good morning," the sheriff said as he came out of his office. "Boys, I hope you were able to sleep last night after all the excitement. Come on in my office."

Matt was surprised when the man from the pickup truck followed them. He sat down in a chair against the wall, leaving the chairs at the sheriff's desk for Grandpa and the boys.

"My wife's bringing in some fresh coffee in a few minutes. That's the advantage of living where you work. Our quarters are out back. My wife does the cooking for us and the prisoners. Most of the prisoners are in for fightin' or drunk drivin'. They serve thirty days or so and then go on their way. A few prisoners, like those we brought in yesterday, are held for the circuit judge. It can get busy around here when circuit court's in session."

A knock at the door interrupted him.

"Here's my wife with the coffee."

When he opened the door, the woman Matt had seen in the outer office came in carrying a tray. The men poured their coffee and settled back in their chairs.

Now," the sheriff said, turning to Grandpa, "how about telling me what happened yesterday?"

"There's not a lot I can tell. Two of my mules were missing, and I'd gone out looking for them. I remembered Matthew saying he'd seen a fellow over at the old creekers' cabin, and I went to take a look. I did a dumb thing and went barging in there and got myself in trouble. If it hadn't been for Matthew and Joshua, I wouldn't be sitting here now. Matthew can tell you more than I can," Grandpa said.

Matt told the sheriff all that had gone on during the past few days and how he had remembered his dad's leather-covered keg and used it to stampede the livestock. The sheriff was taking notes as Grandpa and Matt talked.

"Is there anything else you can think of that you want to add?" he asked, looking at the three of them.

"No, sir," answered Matt and Joshua in unison.

Grandpa just shook his head.

"That was some tale," said the man sitting at the back of the office.

"I thought you'd want to hear this for yourself, Mr. Paulson. That's why I called and asked you to come in," the sheriff said.

He turned to Grandpa. "Mr. Paulson has lost more head of cattle to that bunch than anyone else in the county. He's offered a $500 reward to anyone with information leading to their arrest. You've done better than that. You caught them."

"Well, now, I can't take any credit for that," Grandpa said. "Matthew was way ahead of me. He'd figured out what to do before I got there. In fact, I'd say I just got in the way."

"That's mighty interesting," Mr. Paulson said as he pulled a checkbook out of his overalls pocket and walked to the front of the office. "I'll just make this check out to Matthew. Matthew, what's your full name?"

"Oh no, sir," Matt said. "You'll need to make out two checks."

"How's that?" Mr. Paulson asked. First, Grandpa refused the check, and now Matt wanted two checks.

"I didn't do it by myself. Joshua and I should split the reward. He can add it to the money he's been saving for college.

"Is that a fact?" Mr. Paulson asked, turning to Joshua.

"Yes, sir," Joshua replied. "I'm gonna to be a teacher."

"So you've been saving your money? Do you have a savings account at the bank?"

"No, sir, not yet. I've got $20 at home that I've saved from working this summer. I gave my mama the rest of the money I made."

"Uh-huh. Who're your people?" Mr. Paulson asked.

"John and Annie Williams."

"Oh, yes, I know them. They're good folks," Mr. Paulson said. He paused a moment. "I tell you what I'll do Joshua. I'll open a college fund savings account for you at the Bank of Omaha with a check for $250. After that, anything you put in the account, I'll match."

The room was very quiet.

"Thank you, sir," Joshua said, swallowing hard. He looked rather dazed.

Mr. Paulson looked at the boys. "I don't mind spending money, but I don't want to waste it. I can't think of anything better to spend my money on than education. Now that's settled, I'll need both of your full names so I can make out these checks."

The boys gave Mr. Paulson their names, and he sat at the sheriff's desk and made out the checks.

"You've got a fine grandson here," Mr. Paulson said to Grandpa, shaking Matt's hand as he gave him a check. "I'm sure you'll be putting that in a savings account too."

"Yes, sir. But do you think it would it be all right if I used some of it to buy a baseball mitt?" Matt asked.

Mr. Paulson laughed. "I think that would be money well spent," he said. "We need good teachers, but we need baseball players too."

"By the way, Sheriff, who are the two men who were with the Wilson boys?" Grandpa asked.

"Well, to make a long story short, it seems the boys had been picking up a head or two of cattle every few months and running them up into Arkansas to sell. They made the mistake of stealing a registered beef that had a serial number tattooed inside its upper lip. When they couldn't show ownership papers, the buyer became suspicious.

"It happened the man was this Crawford fellow. It didn't take him long to figure out what the boys were doing. He decided to cut himself and his brother Hank in on the action. He threatened to report the boys to the authorities if they didn't go along with his plan. That's when the rustling activity around here really picked up."

When he finished talking, the sheriff took two small boxes from a drawer in his desk.

"Mr. Paulson, would you ask my deputies John and Pete to step in here for a minute? Ask my wife to come in too."

When everyone was assembled, they waited expectantly as the sheriff cleared his throat and said in a very official tone of voice, "Matthew Morrison and Joshua Williams, please stand."

Not knowing what to expect, Matt and Joshua stood hesitantly.

"This is a special occasion," the sheriff said. "As sheriff of Morris County Texas, I am proud to name Matthew Morrison and Joshua Williams honorary Morris County Texas deputy sheriffs for their bravery and quick thinking that led to the capture of a band of rustlers."

Everyone clapped as the sheriff pinned a badge on each boy's shirt.

After taking a few minutes to congratulate Matt and Joshua, the sheriff's office returned to its usual routine. Mr. Paulson and Grandpa walked out together talking about the weather. Matt had learned people in Texas talk about the weather a lot.

When Matt stepped out on the sidewalk, he looked again at the dilapidated pickup.

"You know, seeing that old truck of his, you'd never think Mr. Paulson is a rich man. And the way he's dresses—he looks like he belongs in a rusty pickup."

"That's true," said Grandpa. "He doesn't go in for show. He spends his money where he thinks it will do the most good."

Grandpa stopped at a filling station on the way out of Daingerfield and bought Dr. Peppers for all of them to celebrate their good fortune.

When Grandpa pulled into the Williams' yard, Joshua jumped out of the truck. "Thanks, thanks a lot," he called over his shoulder as he ran toward the house.

Driving on, they waved to the mailman who had stopped at a row of boxes alongside the road. He had already been to Grandpa's house.

Grandma was standing on the porch when they pulled into the drive. The mail was on the floor at her feet. She was staring at the paper clutched in her hand. Matt could see there were tears on her cheeks when she looked up. Was it a notice from the War Department? Had something happened to his dad?

Chapter 19

Matt sat in the truck. He watched Grandpa hurry up the steps to Grandma. She gave the paper to him with one hand while she wiped tears away with the other. She said something to Grandpa. He put his arm around her as they walked into the house.

They seemed to have forgotten about Matt. It was just as well. His world would stay the same as long as he sat in the truck and didn't know what the postman had brought. He had never thought about how something written on a piece of paper could change his life. It was just a few words. Did he want to know what those words were? He knew the words wouldn't change just because he didn't know. He would have to find out.

The truck was his temporary haven. He left it reluctantly.

Grandpa opened the screened door as he came up the steps.

"Matt, come on in here. Your grandma and I want you to read this letter from your daddy."

It was *from* his dad—not *about* his dad. A feeling of relief swept over him. He hadn't realized how tense and tight his muscles had become until he felt them relax.

"When I saw Grandma crying, I thought something bad had happened." Matt noticed his grandpa looked a little teary too, but he wasn't going to mention it.

"Sometimes I cry when I'm happy," Grandma said. "Just read this, and you'll understand." She held out a letter to Matt.

He took the letter and went to his bedroom to read it.

Dear Mom and Dad,

We've been on the move a lot lately. There have been (here a hole was cut in the letter), but we keep going.

Some things I've seen happen over here have made me realize how lucky I am to have a family waiting for me. Letters from home sure mean a lot. Matt's letters about what he's doing this summer have brought back lots of memories. I could almost imagine myself a kid again in Texas. What great times.

I also remember some unhappy times. I don't regret leaving home and joining the army. I'm just sorry about the way I did it. Looking back, I can't imagine how I could have done such a dumb thing as taking a swing at Dad. Even worse, I've never said, "I'm sorry." That fight, if you could call it that, has stood like a fence between us. We could see each other, but pride and stubbornness wouldn't let either of us open the gate. Dad, I'm sorry for throwing that punch. Mom, I'm sorry for all the heartache I've caused. Now that I have a son of my own, I understand that all you wanted was what you thought was best for me.

I'd better close now and try and get some sleep.
Tell Matt I love him, and I'll write soon.

Your loving son,
Sam

Matt decided his whole family must be a bunch of softies. How else could he explain the tears in his eyes?

After supper, Matt sat on the front porch waiting for the other boys to show up. They had started gathering in the evenings to play baseball. Not that it was much cooler than earlier in the day, but at least, the sun was setting, and there was no glare in the hot summer sky.

Richard, Jim, Jack, Charles, and Tob came up the drive together.

"I think Don is bringing some of the other fellows," Tob said.

Don arrived a few minutes later with the new recruits.

"This here's Sonny and Dale," Don said to Matt. "Sonny's a pretty good pitcher. Not that I don't think you're doing a good job, Tob, but I thought you might could use some relief. You don't want to wear out your pitchin' arm."

No one made a move toward the field after Matt had acknowledged the introductions.

Richard stood with his hands in his back pockets and looked intently at the stick he was pushing around with the toe of his shoe.

Tob threw the baseball into the air and moved the few feet required to catch it.

Sonny took his hat off and wiped his brow on his shirtsleeve.

Jack looked around expectantly.

No one seemed to be in a hurry to start playing ball. Finally, Jim spoke up.

"What's this we hear about you catching the rustlers?"

Matt grinned. Now he knew why they had all come. They might be interested in playing baseball, but what they really wanted was to hear about the rustlers.

"Well, you see, when we were at the Watermelon Festival the other day just before the big storm, Jake and Ray Wilson and some men came to the farm…"

He told the whole adventure just as he had relayed it to the sheriff—with only a little exaggeration. He ended with a flourish—pulling the honorary deputy sheriff badge from his pocket and passing it around.

The boys seemed to be properly impressed with Matt's exploits. They all had questions and talked about what they would have done if they had been there. By the time they finished talking, they were all sure they, too, could be heroes given the opportunity.

It was twilight when they finished talking, but they took to the field and played until dusk settled and the full Texas moon had risen.

Chapter 20

"Joshua, my mom's coming tomorrow," Matt said. "I wrote and told her I could go home on the train by myself, but she wouldn't hear of it. Do you think all mothers are like that, always worrying?"

"Seems to be," Joshua said, adjusting the fishing pole on his shoulder. He and Matt had dug earthworms and caught crickets before heading to the creek. Tall, dry grass brushed against their pants legs as they walked the path. The sky was already a pale, hot washed-out blue, even though the day was young.

"The creek's liable to be low," Joshua said. "Don't 'spect much rain no time soon. More likely not 'til October."

Joshua was right. Only a shallow trickle of water ran along the creek bed. Pools had formed at intervals along the way, offering fish a haven and fisherman an opportunity.

The boys settled on the creek bank and tossed their lines in the water. The small red bobs floated listlessly in the shallow water.

"I don't think anything's gonna bite. The water's too warm," Joshua said as he dropped his hook in another spot. "So you're going home. Think you'll come back next summer?"

"I hope so. I sure want to. I'd like to dig some more for that family treasure." Matt looked at Joshua and grinned.

"Don't look at me. I ain't gonna waste my time digging for your family treasure. Besides, I'm gonna be workin' for Mr. Wright next summer. He said he was countin' on me to be his straw-boss and drive the wagon. Did I tell you I've got a job washin' the storefront

"

windows in town and delivering groceries on the weekend starting next week?"

"That college savings account of yours will be growing like crazy."

"I hope so," Joshua said. "But I've been thinking about being a lawman. When I told Mama, she said it's too dangerous. She said I could do more good teaching, and besides, it's safe in a school. I've got time to think about it."

"Yeah, you have," Matt said. "I'd like to work for Mr. Wright again next summer too. I'll ask him about it before I leave," Matt said.

"You do that. Get your name on the list early. Not that I think he'd turn you down."

"Guess we just as well pull in our lines," Joshua said after they'd watched the bobs for a few more minutes. "Nothin's bitin' today.'"

"You're right. We can leave them to grow 'til next summer."

"I'll be heading on home," Joshua said, gathering the fishing poles and the bate can. "You take care now. I hopes I see you next summer."

He started down the path away from the creek.

"Wait up," Matt called after him.

Joshua stopped and turned around.

"I just wanted to say 'thanks' for—well, for everything," Matt said, extending his hand.

Joshua hesitated. Then a smile slowly spread across his face. "You're mighty welcome," he said as he shook Matt's hand.

Chapter 21

Matt and Grandpa were waiting on the platform when the train pulled into Omaha the next afternoon. Matt jumped down to the roadbed and helped his mother step to the little stool the conductor had placed on the ground. She gave him a hug and then stepped back.

"My goodness, I can't believe how much you've grown," she said. The warmth in her eyes and the smile on her face told him she was pleased with what she saw.

"You've had quite a summer, haven't you? Here I brought you to Texas to escape the danger of polio and you spend the summer chasing gun-toting rustlers."

Matt couldn't tell whether she was upset with him or teasing.

"Now Ann, it wasn't all that bad. Matthew knew just what to do to save the mules and me. He has a good head on his shoulders," Grandpa said as they crossed the highway and headed for the car.

"I'm sure he has. I just don't want it shot off. I have enough to worry about with Sam fighting in Europe. You men have the great adventures while we women stay at home and worry. I'm just glad I didn't know about Matt's run-in with the rustlers until it was all over."

"Mom, you sound like you're mad at me."

"Please, don't misunderstand me. If I sound angry, it's only because I'm afraid something might happen to you. I'm very proud of you and your father."

Conversation lulled on the way to the house. Matt looked out the car window and thought about what his mother had said. She had included him with his father when she said, "You men."

*   *   *

After supper, the family gathered on the front porch. A light breeze made sitting there more comfortable than sitting in the house. The grownups sat in the white rocking chairs Matt had helped Grandpa paint in the barn last week. The chairs had been a surprise for Grandma.

Grandpa turned off the porch light when the June bugs began to make a nuisance of themselves. Matt sat on the top step and listened to the murmur of voices on the porch. Lady was beside him, waiting to have her ears scratched. Duke sprawled on the porch a few feet away.

The accompanying cricket chorus had paused for a moment when Matt's mother said, "Matt, tell me about what all you did this summer."

"Well," Matt said, and he went on to tell about his summer. Everyone laughed when he related his run-in with Roscoe the rooster and his tricking Joshua into helping him dig the garden by saying he was digging for a buried family treasure. No one laughed when he told about Mr. Crawford pointing the rifle at him the first time he went to the creekers' cabin or when he told about capturing the rustlers.

He didn't mention the confrontation he and Grandpa had in the barn. Some things are best left unsaid. Besides, everything had worked out between them. Best of all, things seemed to be working out between Grandpa and his dad.

"You've grown in so many ways this summer," Mom said. "Speaking of growing, I'm sure you've outgrown everything you wore to school last year. Classes will be starting right after Labor Day. That gives us only a few days to do some shopping for you."

Matt groaned inwardly. He'd have to go shopping if he didn't want to wear "highwater pants" to school. Even worse, he could just imagine what the kids in his class would say if he showed up in overalls.

What was really going to be hard to do was adjusting to being back in the city. He had become accustomed to the woods and fields and being able to wander as he pleased.

That reminded him. In the past, the teacher had asked everyone to write an essay about "*What I Did On My Summer Vacation.*" Matt had never had anything interesting to write about. This year would be different. Just wait until the teacher read his essay.

He'd have to think of a good title. How about "*Rounding Up Rustlers in Texas*"? Or maybe "*How I Saved Grandpa From the Rustlers*" or, better yet, "*Rustlers, Rangers, and a Rooster Named Roscoe*" or…

THE END

www.ingramcontent.com/pod-product-compliance
Lightning Source LLC
Chambersburg PA
CBHW030808190726
48285CB00003B/1078